Klutz:

Phoenix Revenge

But Did You Die?

Book 4

Cover artwork by Ana Cruz Arts

www.anacruz-arts.com

Interior formatting by Cauldron Press

www.cauldronpress.ca

A huge thank you to-

Kindled Quill for Developmental Editing.

Maxine Meyer for Copy Editing.

Imogen Evans for Proofreading & Editing.

This book has a cliffhanger. To make up for that, there are some insanely hot bow-chick-a-wow-wow scenes. The men also have some special equipment to make things extra spicy! There are fight scenes and some violence in this book as Ryls and her mates continue their fight against Ridgeforce & Midnight.

KLUTZ

PHOENIX REVENGE

BUT DID YOU DIE?
BOOK 4

SEDONA ASHE

CONTENTS

"*I*'m hurrying, I'm hurrying," I hissed, barely loud enough for the microscopic earbud in my ear to pick up the words.

"You better be. He's going to be back any second." Mace's brogue thickened, which meant he was worried. My stomach dropped to my toes.

"That's not helping, Mace." My hands trembled as I ripped open the tiny foil package. "I'm nervous enough as it is."

"I say we go ahead with Plan B, or C." The higher-than-normal pitch of Knox's voice was a clear indicator he was as freaked out as me.

"Wow. I'm glad you all have so much confidence in me," I grumbled through clenched teeth and bounced anxiously on the edge of the bed.

"Sit down, Knox. We're outnumbered and outgunned. Remember?" Mace snapped. "None of us like this plan, but we all know this is the safest option."

I scoffed. This plan had been my idea. Although when I'd come up with it, I hadn't imagined I'd end up stuffed into a gown with a slit that traveled from the hem of my gown up to my thigh, before moving across my hip and stomach. The bodice of the curve-hugging forest green gown plunged down between my breasts, nearly meeting the leg slit at my belly button. I had bikinis that covered more skin than this dress, and I'd concluded the gown only stayed in place without exposing my lady bits because of some powerful dark magic. It was the only thing that made sense.

When I'd emerged from the bedroom wearing the flimsy material, my mates had taken one look at me and lost their ever-loving minds. There had been a hot minute where I was convinced they were going to run away with me and stash me somewhere far away from the modern world where we could boink like bunnies for eternity and never be discovered. I didn't mind how their plan sounded, but I was determined to finish the whole revenge thing I had planned for Midnight and Ridgeforce.

I had to admit, Xerxes had incredible taste. The silky gown fit in beautifully with the opulent style of Calvin, the leader of Midnight. He'd thrown a party tonight for his investors, probably hoping to distract them from noticing that Midnight was losing both men and money at an alarming rate.

I didn't have an invitation to the ultra-exclusive party, but with my mates' help, it hadn't been difficult to slip through the servant's entrance during the party while the staff was busy serving. And once inside, it hadn't taken long for the host to notice me.

He'd made his way to me almost immediately, and for a terrible moment, I believed he recognized me as the phoenix he was desperately trying to get his hands on. But my disguise worked, or maybe it was just the fact I was dressed up instead of my usual layer of dirt. Calvin had bowed, bending over my hand and kissing it long enough to make my skin crawl.

"The most exquisite woman at my party shouldn't be alone. Join me?" Calvin hadn't waited for an answer, probably because it hadn't really been a request. He was a man used to getting his way.

I'd spent the next four hours at his side, laughing at his horrible jokes and trying to act shy as I dodged his groping hands. If my mates had been able to see the looks Calvin was giving me, they would have stormed inside with claws and magic blazing, not caring about the consequences. Thankfully, they couldn't, and once I finished the mission, I could run into their arms and let them kiss away the feel of Calvin's cringy touch on my skin.

When Calvin had offered me a nightcap, I'd agreed, thankful that our plan was falling into place without a hitch. That was until he led me right past the door of his study and practically dragged me into his bedroom. I'd nearly had a panic attack but was saved when Calvin's phone had rung, and he'd excused himself to take the call.

"Are you okay, Koala Bear?" Mace's voice in my ear

made me jump, pulling me back to my current predicament.

"Yes," I whispered, smiling at the idiotic nickname I secretly adored. "Just trying not to freak out. What did you guys make this package out of? It's more indestructible than me!"

My anxious gaze darted around the room. Everything about it screamed money. You'd have thought the man was Midas with the amount of gold that adorned the room. Golden lamps cast a warm glow into the room and glinted off the shimmering gold silk that covered the king-sized, four-poster bed. Even the curtains were made from a fabric that looked like molten gold.

The room had tall vaulted ceilings, complete with paintings of cherubs floating on fluffy white clouds. Did he seriously get his groove on with those creepy smiles staring down at him? The longer I stared at the strange, old-looking faces on the tiny winged bodies, the more freaked out I became.

I squeaked in fright as Calvin's angry voice sounded in the adjoining room.

"Find their bodies and bring them to me! That little phoenix has cost me too much time and money."

There was a heavy pause before Calvin yelled louder. "I don't care if she's nothing but ash! I don't care if everyone in that compound is ash. I suggest you hire a dump truck and shovels for you and your men and start shoveling. And before you show up here with that truck filled with ash, you'd better find a forensic scientist capable of matching ash to DNA. Otherwise, don't bother coming back. I prefer the phoenix brought to me alive, but since that seems to be beyond our soldiers' skills, I want proof she is dead."

There was a longer silence, and I worked desperately to dump the contents from the tiny foil package.

"No! No more excuses!" he whisper-shouted. "Now, I'm going to enjoy a nice evening with a bombshell from my party. The last few weeks have been insanely stressful, and I need to let off some steam. I'm turning my phone off, and I do not want to be disturbed."

I winced as Anzac released a vehement string of curses. At least, I thought they were curses. It was hard to tell since they were in a language I didn't recognize.

Anzac switched to English, and the earbud crackled at his roar. "Oh, no, he's not—"

"Shut up and sit down, Anzac." Mace barked the order. "We've come this far. Don't blow her mission now. She's got this."

My heart warmed at Mace's confidence in me, but I couldn't help but worry about Anzac. Chewing my bottom lip, I gagged at the chemical taste of the crimson lipstick now coating my tongue. Why did lipstick have to taste so nasty? It was the twenty-first century, for frog's sake. Couldn't science create a strawberry-flavored lipstick for adults?

"You're chewing your bottom lip, aren't you?" Anzac asked in a voice dripping with sensuality. "When you get back here, that lip is mine."

I squeaked and tried to cover it with a cough. After

bringing Anzac back from death, we'd been eager to complete the mate bond.

Finally.

But, as usual, luck had not been on my side. Was having sex with my mate too much to ask?

Apparently.

I'd barely caught my breath from the whole dying thing before we spotted a second team in the distance. None of us had the energy needed to survive another fight, so we'd made like a banana and split.

We left behind nothing but the ashes of our men who'd fallen in battle and the burned remains of the enemy soldiers. Imp had been like a toddler who'd been given permission to use a Sharpie on white walls. She'd burned everything that was flammable, and even a few things that weren't. We didn't stop her until only gray ash covered the earth, knowing it would make it beyond challenging for the enemy to figure out which side had won this battle. It bought us a small window of time. We needed to use that brief respite to strike while our enemies had their defenses relaxed.

Unfortunately, this delayed my bonding with Anzac, and it was causing him a worrisome amount of emotional stress. I wasn't sure if it was the whole coming-back-from-death thing or what, but he was having crazier mood swings than I'd ever experienced… even during my worst period. The dude was a hot-freaking-mess.

One minute, Anzac was covering me in kisses while I tried to focus on planning this mission, and the next, he turned into a prehistoric caveman who could barely speak English. There had also been a few scary minutes where Anzac shifted to his jaguar and couldn't shift back. Let me just say it's a lot harder to travel inconspicuously when you have a larger-than-life jaguar glued to your side and purring louder than a steam engine. Imp, who didn't find the 'cuddle bug' version of Anzac any more appealing than the old Anzac, had been more than happy to zap some sense into him.

Something had to give, and soon. I wasn't sure how long Anzac's body would hold up with the frequent electrical surges, or how long I would last with his teasing but no follow through.

If we could finish this mission, we could take a few days to recover before focusing our attention on our next target. Once the bond between Anzac and me was completed, he should return to normal. Hopefully it worked fast, because I was ready to trade this hormonal and unstable Anzac back in for my dark and brooding Anzac. Butterflies fluttered in my stomach at the thought of mating with Anzac.

"The sooner you finish this mission, the sooner that will happen," I whispered to myself.

Heart in my throat, I quickly squeezed the foil packet. The tiny purple dropped into the sparkling champagne with a faint hiss as it sank to the bottom of the glass.

I could still hear Calvin shouting into his phone as I watched the tiny purple tablet dissolve. At a snail's pace. I chewed on my perfectly manicured thumbnail and tried to remember to breathe. The pill wasn't dissolving fast enough.

I heard the floorboards creak in Calvin's office. He was going to stroll into the bedroom any minute. If he came straight for his glass, he'd have to be blind not to notice the brightly colored pill.

With my eyes watching the doorway between the rooms, I twirled a finger in the glittering golden liquid hurrying along the dissolving process. Calvin shut his phone with a hard snap, and his shadow fell on the doorway. Only psychopaths carried flip phones in this century, although I could see the appeal of getting to end a call with an angry snap. Leaping up, I scurried around the side of the bed and rushed into the bathroom.

"I'm sorry about the interruption." Calvin's voice had every muscle in my body turning to stone. "Where are you going, beautiful?"

Forcing myself to slow my movements, I tried to channel my inner sexy seductress. I leaned playfully against the bathroom door frame, smiling coyly.

"I just wanted to slip into something a little more… revealing." It was an effort to speak with my heart still lodged in my windpipe. I hoped he would mistake my breathless terror for a husky sexiness.

It worked for my mates because a series of groans came through the earpiece.

Determined to sell my sex kitten act, I winked at Calvin and playfully nipped my finger.

The finger that was still damp from stirring the lethal cocktail.

Son-of-a-motherless-goat!

Turning, I shut the bathroom door behind me a little harder than I intended.

"Guys? We have a problem." My tongue felt too big for my mouth and the room tilted at an unnatural angle.

Utter chaos exploded on the other end of the earpiece, but I couldn't make out any of it as my body slumped to the floor.

I sucked donkey balls as a spy.

2

MACE

I stood from my dust-cloth covered chair and stared, slack-jawed at the absolute crap fest happening in the room around me. Calvin lived in a part of the city that was composed of mansions and old money. If we tried to hang out on the quiet, oak-lined street near the mansion, it would have raised suspicion with his guards. That was attention we didn't need.

We'd compromised by hiding out in a home several blocks from Calvin's mansion. The owner had been living abroad for the past decade, according to Xerxes's intel. It was the closest we could get to Ryls while also keeping our vehicle and bodies out of sight.

Watching the men trip over each other, I shook my head. I understood everyone's reaction and could even sympathize, but this chaos wasn't helping. I'd been on countless missions with the jaguars and never believed they'd be capable of losing their heads like this. It was like they were the stars of an amateur comedy hour. I tried to remind myself we were the best agents in the world, but watching my shadow panic left me doubting my memory.

Worst of the entire group was Anzac. The guy hadn't been the same since Ryls brought him back from death, sporting his fiery tattoo. It was still him, but he was unraveling a little more with each hour. Our focus had been on finishing our business with Ridgeforce and Midnight, but I was growing concerned that we needed to turn our attention to fixing Anzac or risk him becoming completely unstable.

A feral jaguar shifter was rare, but not unheard of. If he reached the point of his cat taking over, Anzac regaining control of his mind or body would be all but impossible. I'd never heard of a jaguar shifter coming back from a feral state. While he was struggling with the mate bond pull the most, he wasn't the only one experiencing the strain of the prolonged denial of the bond. Xerxes and I needed to bond with Ryls soon if we wanted to keep from being weakened further, or losing control of our minds.

"Get yer heads out of your arseholes!" I roared above the din.

Every head in the room snapped around to stare at me. Xerxes held a phone to his ear while holding a furious Anzac in a headlock with his other arm. Knox was putting on a shoe—on the wrong foot. Dagger was fighting with his tactical vest, struggling to zip it, even though he'd worn hundreds of these vests over the years. I barely resisted the urge to smack my head.

"Good. Now, calm down so we can figure out how to

help our mate." I crossed my arms over my chest, daring them to argue with me.

Dagger scowled, finally managing to zip his vest. "That's our mate in there, and she isn't responding! How can you tell us to calm down?"

"Because he knows our little bird can handle herself." Jett smirked. He uncoiled himself from where he lurked in the shadows. He and Xerxes hadn't lost their minds when Ryls went silent.

"She's not trained for this type of mission! Who knows what is going on in there!" Anzac snarled.

If the flash of fang and slitted pupils were any indication, he was about two seconds away from shifting into his cat. I rolled my eyes. Great. An overgrown and temperamental pussy-cat was just what my day needed.

"You guys realize she doesn't need us nearly as much as we need her, don't you?" Jett smirked, his lean body maneuvering around the rest of the men as he moved to my side. "It's when things go awry that Ryls shines her brightest."

"Jett's correct. Ryls can handle herself. The last thing she needs is for us to rush in, guns blazing, and turn the situation more volatile. Let's grab our gear and do what we do best—blend into the dark. We need to get close to evaluate what is going on. Got it?"

The guys nodded, wordlessly moving to gather their gear. Xerxes gave me a curt nod before turning back to his phone, his fingers typing furiously on the screen. I didn't waste time trying to understand what the dragon was doing. I'd learned he was unpredictable but highly resourceful. Ryls had chosen well with him.

Grabbing my pack from the floor, I ignored the way my hand shook. As much as I wanted to pretend I was calm and collected, I wasn't. It was against my nature to not rush in after my mate, especially after the last communication she'd sent. But, with Anzac a mess, it forced me to be the voice of reason for the group and keep them from losing it completely.

I had faith in Ryls' abilities, but it didn't stop the fear from chilling my bones. We'd come too close to losing her during the last battle, and that was something I never wanted to experience again. I just needed to learn how to keep her safe from both the world, and, more often than not, herself.

WE CREPT TOWARD THE HOUSE, carefully clearing the expansive manicured lawn inch by inch. This was not the time to make a careless mistake, not with our mate in the house, unarmed.

Well, mostly unarmed if you didn't count the flaming terror that dwelled inside her, or her ability to turn people into a pile of charcoal. While impressive, her skills had proven to be a wildcard. Ryls was just as likely to develop a new ability as she was to call upon an ability she'd used in the past.

That's what makes her so entertaining. Jett's amused chuckle floated through the bond.

It also makes her vulnerable, Dagger countered.

And sexy, Anzac smirked.

The lights cut on and off, giving the mansion an eerie, haunted house vibe. With a final flicker, darkness descended on the house and lawn. I expected a generator to kick on and the lights to blaze back on, but nothing happened. This wasn't normal.

Why weren't guards rushing into position outside the mansion? If they'd hired me to guard the house, I would've immediately suspected an attack was incoming and would have melted into the shadows of the yard to hunt the enemy. I scanned the darkness, but the night was still.

Reaching the house, we pressed our backs against the rough brick walls. I eased myself behind the perfectly trimmed bushes—was that bush shaped like an elephant? I glanced through the window but couldn't see anything through the dense smoke billowing inside the mansion. My grip tightened on my gun. Was that from a raving party, or had something happened? What if Ryls was actually in trouble?

Moving swiftly to the next window, I shot a look inside. Smoke was filling that room as well, and there wasn't a soul rushing around inside. Shouldn't there be guards? Or staff cleaning up from the party? Where was everyone?

Let's move to the main doors of the house. I gave the order through the link, but motioned with my free hand to ensure

Xerxes and Trevor knew the plan. They nodded, following behind us with their guns ready.

We didn't make it more than a dozen steps before the front door flew open with a bone-rattling crash. Smoke poured out, as though the mansion had been holding its breath and could finally exhale. The dark cloud rolled across the porch and down the stairs.

Ryls strode out of the ash plumes like a goddess of death. A pale, filmy material was draped haphazardly around her body. My body grew instantly hard at the sight of her body through the sheer fabric. Lightning streaked and crackled across her skin as though it were daring someone to touch her.

Our girl really knows how to make an entrance, Knox sighed.

You mean an exit, Dagger corrected.

Ryls paused, gripping the fabric tighter between her perfect breasts.

We're here, minx. To the shadows on your left. I spoke through the bond, not wanting to startle her by emerging from the shadows without warning.

Ryls' eyes locked on mine through the darkness and scoffed. "I knew you guys were here."

She coughed from the thickening smoke and drifted toward us down the steps and across the lawn.

Stopping in front of me, she tilted back her head and smirked up at me. "And you're late, again. You guys really need to work on your hero timing."

"You aren't a typical damsel in distress." I chuckled,

remembering the first time we'd organized a rescue on her behalf.

Ryls had not only saved herself, but had rescued Trevor and everyone else being held captive by Ridgeforce. She'd done it a second time when Adam captured her, although, in the chaos, she'd forgotten Trevor. It was only for a millisecond, and we'd circled back around for him like he was a forgotten bag at a grocery store. She's still horrified to this day, but the rest of us still laugh about it when she isn't around.

"I knew you had it under control." Brushing my knuckles along her jawline, I cupped her face. Instant relief rushed through me at the skin-to-skin contact with my mate.

"Yeah, sure." Ryls rolled her beautiful gold eyes. Turning on her heel, she strode toward the front gate. "Let's get out of here. I'm starving!"

We hesitated, eyeing the smoking house. "What about Calvin? His guards? The staff?"

"Calvin's dead, and so are his guards. He'd already sent most of the staff home. The couple who were left are sleeping soundly in the shed out back. Imp made sure they would be out for a while," she called over her shoulder.

That explanation didn't tell us what had happened, leaving me with many more questions. I opened my mouth but closed it when Ryls stumbled over a stick with a yelp.

Xerxes beat me to her side, lifting her easily into his arms. "Are you going to tell us why you are barefoot?"

"And are you wearing a curtain?" Jett snorted.

17

Ryls glanced down at her unusual dress, then lifted her chin. "I'm sure there are other people who've worn clothes from curtains."

"Mm-hm. I can even think of an entire family who wore curtains," Jett snickered.

"The hills are ali—" Knox gave a sing-song whisper.

Dagger flashed a grin and joined in the teasing. "How about, Do-Re-Mi-Fa-So—"

Ryls peeked around Xerxes's arm and scowled. "Don't you start with me!"

"—La-Ti-Do!" Dagger finished with Knox humming along.

"So help me, if you guys don't stop now, you won't be sleeping in my bed for the next month!" Ryls gave a growl that I'm sure she intended to be threatening. It was fricking adorable and extremely close to the sound she'd made when Dagger made her come.

My erection grew painfully hard. It took every ounce of control I possessed not to snatch her from Xerxes and claim her right there on the smoke-filled lawn. Grinding my teeth together, I counted to ten and tried to focus back on the mission.

Take out the target. Check.

Get as far from here as possible. Check.

Still hard. Check.

Focus. Not going so well.

It was better for us to stay 'dead' for a while longer. But studying the smoking house, I suspected our cover was blown. There was nothing to be done about it now, though.

Without a word, we followed Xerxes and Ryls to the SUV we'd left down the street, hidden among the thick shrubbery.

Reaching the vehicle, Anzac shoved past Xerxes to climb into the middle row of the SUV. Once seated, he reached out and plucked Ryls from Xerxes's arms. The dragon's chest rumbled a vicious warning that had every hair on my body rising and the air pulsing with his crackling power. My shadow was feared for our abilities, but Xerxes was a predator on another level.

I'd been so focused on Anzac's instability, I'd missed how Xerxes was being affected by the delay in bonding. With every eye glued on him, Xerxes ran a shaking hand through his hair and straightened his shirt. Ignoring our shocked expressions at his uncharacteristic outrage, Xerxes opened the front passenger door and climbed in.

Eyeing him warily, I moved around to the driver's seat and climbed in. If the unruffable dragon was losing control, we were in a lot worse shape than I'd originally calculated.

"Agreed. I think it's in our best interest to take a vacation." The dragon was back to reading thoughts. "Now."

I nodded stiffly and turned the key to start the vehicle.

"I found a list of Midnight's facilities. There are three of them. Well, two. I already took care of the Austrian facility," Ryls said from Anzac's lap. "We should probably hit them before they discover Calvin is dead."

Xerxes turned to look at her. "It will be dealt with. Jackson has mobilized my other soldiers. They are awaiting my orders."

"But—" Ryls tried to protest.

"No." Xerxes was firm. "For right now, I have this covered. You don't have to fight every battle yourself. I need you to be safe. My dragon is restless, and I can barely control him. We need some downtime. After that, I promise I will follow you into war again, my queen."

It was part order, part plea. I thought Ryls would argue, but glancing in the rearview mirror, I watched her study Xerxes's tense shoulders. Biting her lip, she nodded and sagged back against Anzac's chest.

She'd been laser-focused on seeking justice and getting revenge since the battle. I admired her determination, but even though she'd agreed to the tiny break for Xerxes' sake, the stress was making it difficult for her to eat or sleep, and it was taking a heavy toll on her body.

My gut clenched as I thought about how Ryls had died yet again tonight. Her face was pale, but she wasn't as thin as she'd been this morning. It was a tell that she'd regenerated since I last saw her. The regeneration had restored her body to perfection, but she was going to need a lot of food and rest to make up for the energy she'd lost from the regen.

Xerxes's fingers tapped furiously on his phone and handed it to Ryls. "Here. Tell Jackson what you discovered and everything you can remember. He can get the strike teams sent out so you can stop worrying."

He waited until Ryls was busy talking to Jackson before he spoke to me. "I have a plane landing at a private airstrip thirty minutes from here. It will take us to a private island I own in the Caribbean. Jackson has filed false flight plans to ensure only he and the pilot know where we are going. The pilot has been with me since he was a child and owes me his life. I'm confident he will keep his mouth shut."

"Sounds good." I checked the rearview mirror once more.

Anzac was still holding Ryls tight against his chest, but the rest of the guys had found a way to touch her. We all needed the reassurance that our mate was safe, and if I could, I would be touching her too.

Dagger sat on Anzac's right side, massaging Ryls' bare feet. Trevor sat in the seat behind Anzac, but leaned forward, resting his chin atop the seat so he could play with Ryls' long, crimson hair. Knox sat next to Trevor and leaned forward to hold Ryls' hand. Jett sat on Anzac's left side and stroked her soot-covered cheek.

I would have felt smothered in her position, with all of them crowding around her, but she smiled contentedly. Ryls alternated her focus on each of them, working to calm their inner beasts. Our little mate was perfect and completely selfless.

As my neck grew warm, my heart nearly stopped. A familiar crackling came from far too close to my ear, sending chills down my spine.

"Mace." Xerxes's voice was tense.

I didn't need him to tell me what I already knew. From the corner of my eye, I could see Imp preening and fluffing her fiery feathers from her perch on my shoulder.

"Imp," I croaked a warning. How much did the malicious creature understand? Did she know that if she zapped me now, we'd wreck?

In response, Imp cuddled closer to my neck. If she'd been a lovable parrot, the gesture would have been adorable. Imp wasn't sweet, though. No, she was a creature of darkness who loved making my life a living hell with her tricks.

"Please, be nice," I whispered, not wanting the guys to hear me beg.

Imp's feathers crackled and popped, but she didn't zap me as she fell asleep on my shoulder. I barely moved and resorted to driving with one hand for fear of waking her. It was terrifying.

Once the SUV was out of Calvin's part of town, Dagger handed me a foil-wrapped burger. I unwrapped it suspiciously. "Where did you get this? I thought you guys were staying in the empty house a few streets over?"

I'd been on a mission to execute one of the most powerful men on earth, and my mates decided to go for burgers and french fries without me? Seriously, not cool.

"Is that what took you guys so long? You stopped for a snack break before coming to rescue me? Some heroes you guys are." I gave an unladylike snort, took a bite of the burger, and moaned.

It was incredible and cooked just the way I liked it. My mates preferred thick burgers on the rare side and dripping with juices. But my favorite was when the burger patty was smashed flat and allowed to sizzle until the meat was crispy. Finish it off with extra cheese and double the sauce, and I was one happy phoenix.

"Of course we didn't stop to eat on our way!" Anzac protested.

I lifted a brow and took another bite of the burger.

"I just thought you might want it!" Dagger avoided my gaze and rubbed the back of his neck. "While you were dancing with Calvin, a.k.a. Mr. Wandering hands, I did a quick run to grab you a burger."

It was thoughtful, so why was he acting guilty? Taking another bite, I studied him, trying to work out the puzzle.

"He thought you were going to die, and he knew you would be hungry when you came back," Xerxes answered my unspoken question without bothering to look up from his phone.

"Why'd you have to tell her that?" Dagger demanded.

Xerxes shrugged. His face showed no emotion except for the tiny tilt at the corner of his mouth. He probably found this amusing because he'd wanted to do the same thing, but Dagger had simply beaten him to it, and now Xerxes was happily throwing Dagger under the bus just to mess with him.

Xerxes was still getting used to being part of our odd little family, and it thrilled me to know he'd grown comfortable enough to enjoy bantering with the guys. It was endearing, but I hid my smile, not wanting to let my mates off the hook too easily.

"Did anyone here believe I would make it through the mission without dying?"

Trevor and Mace raised their hands, while the rest of the guys avoided looking at me.

Mace caught sight of Trevor's raised hand in the rearview mirror, and dark mischief danced in his emerald green eyes. "That's not entirely truthful. Is it, Gryphon?"

His Scottish brogue was thick, and I had to bite my cheek to keep from grinning. I loved when my red-headed giant slipped deeper into the sexy accent of his homeland.

Trevor muttered a curse under his breath and lowered his hand.

"That's better." Mace laughed, and his eyes caught mine as he explained. "We all cast a vote. Trevor believed you would survive the mission, but he bet you would die after you completed it. Like tripping down the stairs as you left and being impaled by the elephant bush."

"Seriously, Trevor?" Wrinkling my nose, I stuck my tongue out at him. "That's just insulting."

I didn't get to see his reaction because Anzac bent down his head and captured my tongue between his teeth in a single swift movement. Before I could pull it back, he'd sucked it inside his mouth. His tongue twisted around mine in a sensual dance. Heat bloomed in my chest. When he released me, I gasped for air.

My chest burned, pushing me to be with my mate. The same desperate need shimmered in Anzac's hooded eyes. How much longer could we hold off the urge to finish the bond? Anzac was honoring my wish to wait for a quiet, romantic moment to mate. But the need was beginning to drown out human logic, and seriously, the backseat of a car was looking pretty good right now.

Cheeks flaming in both desire and embarrassment, and

not sure what to do with myself, I attempted to take another bite of my burger before remembering the task was easier if I put my tongue back in my mouth first.

"By the way, where is Jackson?" It had surprised me he wasn't with my guys, although it was a relief he hadn't witnessed the whole curtain-fashion-faux-pas thing.

"There were a few things I needed to take care of. I didn't trust anyone else to do it, so he's handling it. We will meet up with him in a few days." Xerxes gave me a lop-sided smile.

I couldn't help but be worried about Jackson, but I was also relieved. Getting some time alone with my mates was long overdue. Leaning back against Anzac, I savored my burger.

"I know you're tired, but we need to be briefed on what went down tonight." Jett's lips twisted in an apologetic smile.

I held up a finger as I tried to chew and swallow the overly large bite of my hamburger I'd bitten off. They were super soldiers, and for them, the mission always came first in their minds. The burger was delicious, and I wanted to give it my undivided attention, but the guys had been patient.

"Everything went fine—at first. Once we made it to the bedroom, I slipped the pill into the champagne without Calvin noticing. The problem was, it didn't dissolve fast enough, and I worried Calvin would spot it fizzing at the bottom of the glass. "Sooo..." Drawing out the word, I stalled. I wasn't eager to admit to the next part of the tale.

"Deciding I needed to hurry the process along, I gave it a quick stir with my finger."

In unison, the entire car groaned. Drama queens. They should be used to this nonsense by now. Besides, I was the one who had to do the actual dying and coming back... inconveniently naked.

"Please, please," Dagger begged. "Tell me you did not stir a poison with your finger and then stick that same finger in your mouth!"

Saying nothing, I stuffed my mouth with a massive bite of the burger.

Jett tugged gently on a strand of hair, his face alight with amusement. "You are many things, little bird, but perhaps being a spy isn't one of them."

"Calvin's dead, and so are his men. So I got the job done, didn't I?" I sighed in annoyance.

"We don't know. Did you?" Mace asked, catching my eyes in the rearview mirror.

"Of course I did," I grumbled, mentally willing Imp to fry his sexy butt. Like the traitor she was, she ignored me and cuddled up closer to him.

"What happened after you decided to taste test the toxin?" Dagger prodded, trying to get me back on track.

"I made it to the bathroom and locked the door behind me. That's when I told you guys we had a problem."

Trevor pushed the burger toward my mouth, reminding me to eat. "And Calvin didn't question what you were doing?"

Swallowing a quick bite, I shrugged. "I guess he liked

27

the idea of me getting sexy for him, because no, he didn't try to get into the bathroom. After I contacted you guys, I collapsed onto the floor."

Knowing they didn't like when I died, I hurried to gloss over the whole death thing. "As usual, I came to... dressed in my birthday suit, and peeked open the door to see if Calvin was still waiting."

"Was he?" Knox had his fists clenched. "If you tell me he was waiting for you—"

"He wasn't. He was dead. Calvin must have helped himself to his champagne while waiting for me. The toxin did its job."

"Then what? You yanked the curtain off the window and came out to meet us? Where was everybody?"

"Calvin had already ordered the guards to leave him alone and give us privacy, so the house was mostly empty. The few guards still on duty were watching TV in the security room. Imp, deciding to play some fiery leapfrog, knocked out the guards before they even knew what was going on. Once they were out cold, it wasn't a problem to set fire to that room. If they find the bodies and perform autopsies, the lungs will have smoke showing the guards inhaled, and there wouldn't be signs of a struggle. It will look like they didn't realize there was a fire and inhaled too much smoke."

Xerxes turned in the seat to look at me. "What about the kitchen staff?"

"Only two ladies were still in the kitchen cleaning up the party mess. Before they could spot me, Imp gave them a little zap-nap. I pulled them to the little shed out back. They're going to wake up with a terrible headache, but they'll be fine."

Anzac's brow creased. "Investigators aren't stupid. They're going to realize Calvin was poisoned. It won't take them long to suspect you."

I shook my head. "I dropped the glass into the dishwasher with the rest of the glasses. Even if they suspected it, they'd have trouble locating his glass among the hundreds of glasses strewn about the kitchen and dining area."

"Okay, but what about the women? Unless Imp scrambled their memories, they'll know something weird happened." Knox drummed his fingers on his thigh.

I narrowed my eyes at him. Was it so hard to believe I did a good job? "I hauled several garbage bags outside and placed them near the women. They are going to wake up confused, but will think they were taking out the trash, and the timing saved their lives."

Not giving them time to ask, I added, "After setting fire to various rooms, I made my way out the front door to be rescued. Late. Again." I loved reminding them.

Seriously, I know they were super-talented secret agents, but couldn't they give me a little credit? Putting aside the whole dying thing, I'd pulled this off like a rockstar. Just call me Phoenix, Amaryllis Phoenix. And after tonight, I prefer my drinks shaken, not stirred.

Xerxes's bark of laughter gave me a jump scare. The naughty dragon had been reading my thoughts. He wanted to play this game? Bring it. I started thinking about having sex with him, visualizing the explicit act in boner-inducing high-def detail. Xerxes choked on his laughter and shifted his hips to adjust his raging hard-on.

That's what I thought. You aren't ready to play in my mind, Grasshopper, I purred in his mind. Wondering how far my abilities could go, I mentally brushed my fingers across the bulge in his dark pants. Would Xerxes be able to feel the invisible touch?

Xerxes's body stiffened, and he hissed out a harsh breath.

Oh, yes. He'd definitely felt that. Smiling like the Cheshire cat, I wrapped my fingers around his erection and squeezed—not hard enough to hurt him, but enough to make sure he knew who was in control. Xerxes's head fell back against the headrest, and his body trembled. Checkmate, baby.

Dagger snapped me from the dangerous new game I was playing. "Yeah, well. I don't understand why you even had to place yourself in such a dangerous situation. Calvin is a criminal. Letting him get you alone was a death wish."

Refocusing, I tried to pull my thoughts together—out of Xerxes's mind and pants. He let out a whimpering groan.

"You know exactly why I did what I did. If I'd found the opportunity to slip it into his drink during the party, I would have. But the man never let go of his glass, making that impossible. If I had poisoned the bottle the servants had been serving Calvin from, they might have served other guests with that same tainted bottle."

It was why I waited. Not wanting innocent house guests or servants to be casualties for being in the wrong place at the wrong time. There were several people at the party who deserved to die. But how could I live with myself if, in my mission to get revenge, I ended up killing other innocents? This was about getting justice, not creating more hurt in the world.

"I still think the mansion burning in a fire will tip off investigators to the fact you were there and that you're still alive. Fire is kinda your calling card."

"They might, but I was careful to not put too much power into the fire. It should look like a normal electrical fire. Hopefully, it was enough to buy us another week." If we were lucky. Luck wasn't something I put much faith in, though.

Jett sighed. "There's another problem, Ryls. The mansion has security feeds that are backed up to the servers in Calvin's office downtown. One of the first things investigators will do is check the house security feeds. They are going to see you with Calvin, and then see you taking out the guards and starting the fire. Even dressed up, wearing a wig, and covered in makeup, it won't take long for them to discover your identity."

"Already taken care of." Using my free hand, the one not holding my burger, I shot a finger gun at Jett while clicking my tongue. "Who said I couldn't be a spy?"

Jett started to protest, but I held up my hand.

"Imp fried something in the electronics when we arrived. I'm not sure of the details other than it had to do with how the footage was being recorded, but I'm confident the video feeds being transmitted to the servers outside the mansion were blank."

Mace eyed the pint-sized troublemaker preening on his shoulder with something close to respect. "It sounds like ye caused more than your fair share of chaos tonight," he murmured.

Imp gave a happy little trill. To my utter shock, Mace reached up a finger and brushed through Imp's sparkling feathers.

"We're all going to die," Knox whispered, horror causing his voice to crack.

He assumed, just like the rest of us, that Imp was about to knock Mace the frickity-frack out and kill us all in the process.

Imp wove herself around Mace's neck like a cat weaving between its beloved owner's legs. She then cuddled up against his neck, puffing out her feathers until her head nearly disappeared into the fiery ball. She looked like an adorably chubby 'birb' drawing, rather than a regal harbinger of magical malice.

This had been a weird day, but frankly, Mace petting Imp took the cake.

Crisis averted, the guys slowly released their death grips from the seats and door handles they'd used to brace themselves and let out the breaths they'd been holding.

Not knowing what to say, I took another bite of my delectable burger and watched the headlights illuminate the dark road stretching out in front of us.

*A*nzac refused to put me down and carried me onto the plane. My cheeks warmed with a blush as the pilot greeted us. I was dressed in a curtain, for Pete's sake.

"And you look stunning," Xerxes murmured, following behind Anzac.

These men needed their eyes checked. I wasn't an idiot. I knew I looked like a hot mess. It was kind of sweet to have them so in love they thought I was beautiful all the time.

Anzac moved down the aisle to a window seat. My heart lurched, and my throat squeezed shut. I didn't think I would ever fly again without feeling panic. I'd managed to experience both a helicopter and a plane crash in the past months. I wasn't eager to live through yet another crash.

Instead of sitting me in my own chair, Anzac sat down, holding me on his lap. "It's okay, Ryls. We're safe," Anzac murmured into my hair. His arms tightened around me, cradling me against his chest.

They were the first words he'd spoken to me since I'd heard him in my earpiece earlier that evening.

"Logically, my brain knows that, but my body has its doubts," I whispered.

Yeah, dying sucked, but it was manageable. When my men were in jeopardy, that's when I had a serious problem.

The pilot's disembodied voice crackled through the speakers, letting us know the plane was preparing for take-off. My eyes stung with unshed tears and my lungs refused to work. I could do this. It would be fine, right?

Panic bubbled inside me like a fourth-grade science volcano experiment gone wrong. Or like when you put too much detergent in a washing machine and the entire floor ends up covered with an explosion of bubbles. Or like how you should never make your own homemade cleaners using both ammonia and bleach. Not that I had personal experience with any of those things.

Xerxes barked a laugh and tried to cover with a fake cough. I wasn't fooled, though. He'd been listening to my thoughts again. If I wasn't on the verge of panicking, I'd mess with his mind, but I was too busy trying to not think about the roaring of the plane's engines as it picked up speed.

Anzac shifted me in his arms, sitting me up on his lap to face him. The change of position was so smooth and swift that I could only gasp in surprise. He lost no time in taking advantage of my open mouth. Anzac sucked my lip between his lips. Gentle and teasing. This time when I

34

gasped, it was from lust. His tongue slid along my lip before his mouth fully claimed mine.

His hand cupped my jaw, then moved to the back of my neck. Using his hold on my neck, he angled my neck to give him more control of the kiss. I moaned into his mouth, and he swallowed the sound like a man starving. When the plane jerked and bounced, lifting off from the runway, my body trembled, and my heart beat harder.

I tried to turn my head to look out the oval window into the darkness, but Anzac's fingers tightened around the back of my neck. "Don't. Focus on me."

Anzac's free hand brushed against my breast, the gauzy curtain providing very little barrier between his hungry touch and my flushed skin. The rough, calloused skin of his thumb teased across my nipple. Unable to stop myself, I whimpered. He wasn't the only one struggling with the incessant call of the mate bond.

I needed his touch, his body, his bite. He already bore my mark on the fiery tattoo on his back. Now, I wanted to feel him claim my body.

"We need to stop," I managed between kisses.

"No, we don't." Anzac's hand trailed down my ribs and over the curve of my hip.

I didn't want to stop, but I'd been the one to refuse my first time with Anzac being a quickie. I'd wanted to wait for a better time... and a bed. Did he really want to complete the bond on an airplane with a large audience? This was hot a sin, but didn't he want to wait for a more romantic moment?

This is romantic, Anzac purred in my mind while his finger traveled lower until he was teasing my slick entrance. *I can't think of anything sexier than ripping off that drape and burying my cock inside you. I want to hear you scream my name and feel your nails scratch my skin as I stretch you and fill you.*

I shivered. We had different ideas about what constituted a romantic moment, but I found myself eager to try out his version. Mates should always be open to each other's ideas, right?

I want that, I confessed, hating that my cheeks were probably turning a brighter red than my hair.

That was all the permission—or perhaps encouragement —Anzac needed. With a growl, he yanked away the flimsy curtain, exposing my bare breasts. He wasted no time in devouring first one breast and then the other, his rough tongue lapping across my nipples and sending shockwaves directly to my core.

While his mouth was busy with my breasts, his hand moved between our bodies. Anzac's knuckles inadvertently rubbed against my aching entrance as he unbuckled his pants and freed himself from the confines of the dark black jeans. I fought the urge to rock against him, desperate for friction against my aching heat.

I've got you, Anzac promised, and without warning, he plunged two fingers inside me. He wasn't gentle, and I didn't want him to be. His fingers thrust hard into me, stroking my walls and rubbing roughly against the bundle of nerves begging for his undivided attention.

My thighs quivered, and I tried to remember how to breathe. Anzac's mouth moved from my mouth, traveling the length of my jaw and down my neck. His teeth pressed into my neck. He didn't pierce my skin, but he was letting me know he could at any moment. It was a delicious promise, and a surge of anticipation shot through me.

"Please. I can't wait any longer." I wasn't too proud to beg.

You aren't in charge. Anzac's teeth pressed a little hard, and his fingers flicked against my aching nub. *First, you will come on my fingers. I want to feel your body clench around my hand as I make you orgasm.*

As though unable to deny him, I came apart. My body trembled as my release tore through me and coated his fingers with the evidence of my desire. Anzac released his hold on my neck and slipped his fingers from my silky channel.

I watched through hooded eyes as he lifted his slick fingers and licked them clean, never once breaking eye contact with me. It was one of the hottest things I'd ever witnessed, and my stomach clenched as a new, more powerful need stirred inside me. I needed more of him. All of him.

"Either use that magic wand of yours for good, or I am going to find another one to take a ride on." I meant for it to sound like an order, but it came out in a breathless plea.

Several of my mates' hands shot into the air, offering themselves as tribute. I glanced around the small plane, taking in the dark, hungry faces of my mates.

Even Trevor, who was still shy about group activities when it came to sex, watched us with his hand tightly gripping the hard bulge in his combat pants.

How was I so lucky to have such dangerously sexy mates? How could these powerful men look at me with so much desire?

"Right now, you are mine and no one else's." Anzac didn't wait for my response.

Grabbing my hips, Anzac lifted me off his lap and teased my entrance with the head of his stiff erection. I closed my eyes and expected him to thrust himself inside, but he didn't move.

"Amaryllis?" There was a wistful note in Anzac's voice.

My eyelids popped open, and I gasped at Anzac's glowing irises. The crystal blue depths swirled with pain, need, sorrow, desire, regret, hope, and so much love it knocked the wind from my lungs like a physical blow.

"I've said it before, but I am so sorry—"

I pressed a finger to his lips. "Anzac, we've been over this so many times. It's in the past."

Anzac sucked my finger into his mouth. His tongue swirled around it before he gave it a playful nip. "Yes, we have. But I need you to know that walking away from you on that beach will always be the biggest regret of my life. I treated you despicably. If only I'd claimed you like my jaguar wanted. He knew from the moment you saved us that you were a treasure, a mate far better than what we deserved."

The day we'd crashed onto the beach had been one of

the worst of my life, and it was nice to hear him admit how badly he'd messed up. But seriously, this was not the time. I didn't want a stroll down memory lane; I wanted to complete a long overdue bonding with my mate.

Leaning forward, I kissed Anzac, pouring my love into the kiss. When I pulled away, I caught his face between my hands, forcing him to meet my gaze.

"I've already forgiven you. You were willing to give your life to try and save mine. I desperately want you as my bonded mate, Anzac. Now, could you please stop talking and claim me?" I wasn't ashamed to beg.

He was surprisingly gentle as he lowered me inch by inch down his thick girth. Closing my eyes, I forced my muscles to relax and accept his length. Once he was buried as deep as my body could take him, Anzac held still, giving me time to adjust.

After my body had adjusted to being stretched by his thick erection, I needed him to move.

He might have tried to keep talking, but the plane hit a sudden patch of turbulence, causing my body to lift from his lap and then come down hard. Thanks to his length and his hands gripping my hips, I stayed firmly impaled on his manhood. We moaned simultaneously at the rough friction. That was all the encouragement he needed, and without any further begging on my part, Anzac lifted me from his lap and brought me down hard a second and then a third time.

My vision blurred, and fire burned along every nerve ending. A ravenous hunger boiled inside me. Ignoring the way my knees bumped against the armrest, I wrapped my arms around Anzac's neck and pressed our bodies together. His tongue delved between my parted lips while his erection thrust into the silken heat between my legs.

He was claiming every part of me, and still, I wanted more. Using what leverage I could gain with my arms around his neck and my knees on the soft leather of the airplane seat, I pushed myself up and down Anzac's length at a frantic pace. I had taken control, and it excited the alpha in him, driving him to dominate me.

It didn't matter to me which of us was in control, but when Anzac snarled and pounded into me with the force of a jackhammer, I was more than happy to let him take the lead.

I forgot how to think, how to breathe, how to do anything other than hang on for the ride of my life. Anzac's fangs sank into my neck, and I cried out. Chills raced across my skin, and my body flushed with the dark pleasure rising inside me, a sign of my coming release.

Gritting my teeth, I tried to keep them from clattering together while Anzac released all his pent-up desire on my body. I groaned as the tightness between my legs turned to a pinch and then a slight burn. The change was so gradual that I didn't notice right away. Not until Anzac slowed a fraction to force himself into me.

What had happened? One minute he fit, and the next he was too big.

I whimpered at a sharp twinge of pain.

"Anzac," Mace warned, his voice sounding a million miles away.

Anzac rumbled a warning of his own and shoved his erection deep inside me. With a burst of clarity, I realized what was happening. Anzac was losing control of his jaguar and his humanity. His beast was pushing him to mate me in the way of his species... something the rest of my jaguar mates had done their best to avoid or hold back.

I'd known that Anzac and Mace would likely have the hardest time maintaining control, and that mating with them might be more painful since my body hadn't been designed to take a barbed penis. It hadn't worried me as much as it worried my mates, though. The way I saw it, worst-case scenario, I died. Death by dick wasn't the worst way to go.

Anzac forced his quickly swelling erection inside me. The spiked barbs that covered that velvet steel of his length were still only rounded bumps, and they massaged my tight walls. What I hadn't counted on was the instantaneous orgasm that ripped through me as, one after another, the rounded barbs pressed against my g-spot.

I screamed his name while my body trembled, but Anzac wasn't finished with me. Not by a long shot.

Anzac yanked himself from inside me and buried himself deep in a single rough stroke, the barbs massaging while sliding against me. Even through the haze, I could tell the barbs protruded more. I was still riding the waves of pleasure from my first orgasm when Anzac circled his hips beneath me. Reality shattered around me as he tore a second orgasm from me.

I screamed until my throat ached. Anzac didn't stop. He continued moving his hips beneath me like he was a freaking belly dancer. How he was able to move like that while sitting down seemed more supernatural than his ability to shift into a giant kitty.

Sweat soaked my body, and my stomach twisted in anxiety as the barbs dug their rounded tips into me. My third orgasm tore through me, far stronger than the first two. I would have collapsed if Anzac hadn't been supporting me. I sobbed from the intensity of the pleasure.

Anzac's fingers dug into my hips, sending a quick shock of pain as his nails sharpened. He was struggling, but lost in a sea of bliss, I was in no condition to calm him down.

"Anzac!" Mace's sharp tone floated through my numbed mind.

Anzac pulled his fangs from my neck, and his outraged roar echoed through the plane. The threat of his mate being taken from him during the claiming snapped his wavering control. Anzac's instincts took over, and I was enthusiastically all for it.

With a last hard thrust, Anzac plunged inside me, his round-tipped barbs digging into my walls. Sinking his fangs into my flesh a second time, he pulled his hips back slightly, and the barbs anchored themselves inside me, pinning us together.

I screamed as the mother of all orgasms forcibly ripped my soul from my body. My soul did the hokey-pokey, turned itself around, and finished by stuffing itself back inside my shuddering body.

It was too much for Anzac and, releasing my neck, he roared his release. My body clenched around his member, allowing me to feel every sensation as his erection pulsed, and he coated me with his molten release.

With every ounce of energy drained from my body, my eyelids grew heavy. I relaxed against Anzac's chest, fighting the need to sleep.

"Rest. I've got you." Anzac held me to him, a soothing purr rumbling in his chest beneath my ear. "For as long as I breathe, I'll take care of you."

My heart was full, and all the old hurts had been healed. Tilting my head up, I pressed a soft kiss to his neck. Cuddled in his arms, I didn't even care as turbulence continued to toss the tiny plane about. I was happy.

"I love you, Anzac." My words were little more than a soft whisper as his purr lulled me to sleep.

Anzac's arms tightened around me, and his purr grew louder. "I love you more, Koala Bear."

As I fell into a dreamless sleep, something wet splashed against my cheek. If it had been another of my mates holding me, I would have believed it was a tear.

a few hours later, I was walking hand in hand with Trevor on a white, sandy beach. The beautiful turquoise water shimmered in the bright morning sunshine. Gentle waves lapped on the shore, and tiny crabs darted through the foamy bubbles left behind. Birds in every color of the rainbow hopped from branch to branch in the thick foliage growing off to our left.

We'd left the men relaxing in the hand-woven hammocks stretched between the trees in the villa's court-yard. The home was much smaller than Xerxes's sprawling mansion in Mexico, but I secretly liked the cozy island home more. It had a homey feeling that had me imagining a normal life without assassins or government conspiracies, but that life seemed to be far away.

I was thankful for the chance to have a bit of alone time with Trevor. All my mates craved time with me, and since they didn't mind sharing, there was very little one-on-one time with each mate. They were purposefully giving Trevor this time alone with me. It was incredibly sweet to know.

My gryphon and I hadn't been able to talk much about his trip home with the insane chaos of the past few days. I swung our interlaced hands between us, happiness warming my chest. At nearly six and a half feet tall, compared to my five-foot height, I probably looked like an elf walking along beside him.

I craned my neck to look up at Trevor, admiring his bronze skin and his white hair that fell in a long braid down his back. The sun glinted on his golden strands of hair that weaved through the pale hair. I couldn't believe he was the same pale, thin man I'd met in the lab. These days he was the picture of health, and I struggled to believe he was really mine.

"You wish to ask me something," Trevor stated, his lips tilting in a gentle smile. "So ask."

"How do you know that?" I squinted up at him, hoping my cheeks weren't giving away my embarrassment.

"I can feel your curiosity and your reluctance. You want to ask me something, but you're worried about doing so. What is it, my love?" He lifted our intertwined hands and brushed a kiss along the back of my hand.

"I wanted to know—" I twisted a lock of hair around my finger. It was a nervous gesture, and forcing myself to stop, I took a deep breath and blurted it out. "I wanted to know if you would show your gryphon to me. Your entire gryphon, not just your wings."

Trevor's eyes widened in surprise. "You want me to shift? Here? Now?"

"Yes!" I shouted. Lowering my voice, I added belatedly, "Please? You were amazing during the battle—and terrifying—but mostly amazing. I was dying to touch your feathers, but we were kind of busy with the whole fighting-for-our-life thing."

I struggled to hold back my enthusiasm. Seeing the men in all their forms was important to me, and I held my breath, waiting for his response.

Trevor's eyes lit with excitement. "I didn't think you'd be interested in my gryphon form. It would be an honor to shift for my mate."

I did a happy dance that made Trevor bark out a laugh. Pulling my hand free of his, I made a shooing motion. "Well, go on! Chop, chop. Time's a wastin'."

Trevor bent and kissed my cheek. He shook his head over my silliness, but I didn't miss the way he beamed with pride. Trevor jogged a few yards down the beach. He stopped, turning toward me with a hesitant look on his face. "Ryls? I need to explain something about my gryphon before I shift."

"Okay?" I drew out the word, curious about what he was suddenly so concerned about.

Trevor scratched at the back of his neck. "My beast is, well, different from me."

I raised a brow. "I'm confused, Trev. Different, how?"

"You know how Knox is outgoing and goofy?" At my nod, he continued. "My gryphon could give Knox a run for his money. In my shifted form, I've been told I'm 'exuberant.' Everything is a game, and I've been told I can be a bit much. Like an overgrown puppy without manners."

His bronzed cheeks turned red, as though he'd just told me a humiliating secret.

It took some time for my brain to process what he was saying. When the pieces clicked into place, a laugh escaped me. Just the thought of my gentle, calm, regal, and quiet mate turning into his exact opposite was a hilarious mental image.

Now I was even more excited. "What are you waiting on? Hurry up, buttercup!" I plopped down on the sand and stared intently, waiting for the show to start.

Trevor's muscles relaxed, the tension draining away. His eyes glowed in excitement, and a radiant smile lit his face. This man, with the face and body of a fallen angel, wanted to show off for me.

Butterflies took flight in my stomach, and I could hardly breathe as I awaited his shift. With a soft hum, magic blurred across his skin like a mirage in the desert. Reality twisted as the impossible became possible. In only a few seconds, a gryphon stood in front of me.

His hind legs were that of a muscular lion, a king among predators on Earth. In contrast, his powerful front legs were that of a bird of prey, a ruler of the sky. Razor sharp claws dug into the sand from his back legs, and gold-tipped talons glinted in the sun on his front legs.

A salty breeze drifted to shore, ruffling through his fur and the feathers of his wings. The gold-dipped tips of each feather caught the light, sparkling like stars against a dark chocolate background.

If I thought he was big in the sky, he was positively monstrous on the ground, and I had no idea what he'd been embarrassed about. He looked majestic and regal.

"Shut the front door!" I squeaked. "You're nearly the size of an elephant!"

The gryphon approached, opened his beak, and screamed, blowing my hair crazily around my face. I should've been scared, but it was hard to feel fear when you had looked death in the face so many times. Been there, done that... and will probably do it again in the near future.

I tapped my chin thoughtfully. "Hm. I take it you don't like being called an elephant?"

The gryphon violently shook his head from side to side. Narrowing his large eyes, he fluffed out his feathers in disgruntled irritation. I couldn't stop my giggle—so much for regal. It was the same gesture Imp made when annoyed by one of the guys.

"Fine, fine. I won't compare you to an elephant again." *To your face, anyway.*

Trevor pinned his feathery ears back, flattening them against his head. With a huff, he sat back on his hunches.

I took a tentative step forward, and then another. The gryphon's eyes focused on me with the sharp focus of a bird of prey. That was when I should've shown a bit more common sense and backed away, but I couldn't. My mind flashed back to the first time Knox had approached me in his jaguar form. I'd intensely wanted to pet his silky soft fur, even knowing it'd likely lead to my death.

Trevor's ears popped forward, and his head tilted to the side like the curious puppy he warned me about. His pupils rounded as he watched me. When I didn't move, he rolled onto his back, spread his wings, and wiggled around in the sand. Sand showered down around him. The giant gryphon playing on the beach was one of the strangest and cutest things I'd ever seen.

How could I resist? Besides, it wouldn't be the first time I died petting something adorable. My bird-kitty wanted belly rubs... and I wasn't strong enough to say no.

"Ah, fluffin' heck!" Rushing forward, I buried my hands into the feathery down of his belly.

Trevor stiffened slightly as I leaned down and rubbed my cheek against his soft belly feathers. He was far too large for my arms to reach around even his chest, but I gave it my best effort. I touched everywhere I could reach.

"You are amazing, Trevor." I continued to explore his gryphon body.

Without warning, his wing smacked my butt, tossing me into the air. Landing on his stomach, I gave a shocked yelp. I waited to see what he would do next, but his talons distracted me. I ran my hands across each one. The claws were easily the length of one of my hands, and the nails appeared to be made from gold. No wonder he'd been able to rip the helicopters apart with so little effort!

"It was incredible the way you rushed into battle, ready

to eat those helicopters like they were nothing but toys," I said conversationally while stroking his feathers.

Trevor didn't respond, but it didn't stop me from talking.

"I was so worried they were going to kill everyone on the ground. Then you swooped in and wrecked their plan. It was epic!"

Trevor cocked his head to the side, listening intently as I talked. Occasionally he'd give a soft coo that was absurdly cute. One minute I was lying on his wide feathered chest; the next he rolled over. I landed on the ground with a thud, even though the sand helped cushion my impact.

The gryphon stood to his feet, stretched like a cat, and then moved to stand over me. Was the beast in control, or was Trevor in control? Or maybe they shared control in this form? I hated how lacking my knowledge was about gryphons. I knew the jaguars' beasts could control the abilities both in the cat and human forms, but how much control did Trevor have when he shifted? There was so much I needed to learn about all my mates.

The gryphon eyed me with a look that I'd seen many times on my own face. Hunger. He moved his front legs closer, pinning me between them. I laid still, knowing we were playing a dangerous game. Trevor could accidentally crush me in this form with incredible ease. If he so much as twitched, he could pierce me with a single talon, and I'd be dead—at least for a minute or two.

There were worse ways to die, though. I could easily name ten or fifteen off the top of my head. It was doubtful that Trevor could emotionally handle living with the memory of unaliving me. The smart thing would be to wiggle away without exciting the predator's instincts. But playing with death in the form of a bird-kitty was far too enticing.

"Such a pretty bird," I praised in the same tone I used on the Macaw at the zoo.

The gryphon's pupils thinned to slits, and his ears flattened.

"Oh? Did I hurt the pretty bird's feelings?" I teased, excitement bubbling inside me.

Trevor stomped his gold-tipped talons into the sand near my head. The ground reverberated under my body from his massive body. That's when I noticed something I'd missed at first…

"You have a tail!" I exclaimed and wiggled around until I could crawl under his body.

Popping up behind him, I watched the lion's tail flick back and forth in irritation. Grabbing the fluffy tuft on the end of his tail, I brushed the long fur.

The gryphon bent down its great head, watching me between his legs. His ears were forward, and his head tilted in bewildered curiosity. It was like he'd never seen a creature quite like me before.

With surprising gracefulness, Trevor spun around. I'd still been holding his tail in a firm grip, and the sudden movement jerked me off my feet, sending me face-planting in the sand. Dang. Did all gryphons toss their mates around?

With a worried rumble, Trevor's cool beak pressed against my neck. He nuzzled me, trying to push me up and make sure I was unharmed.

Groaning, I rolled over. "I'm fine, I'm fine."

Trevor wasn't convinced by my wheezing reassurance, and he continued to nuzzle me. His beak pressed to my skin, checking every bone in my body. Finally satisfied I was fine, Trevor pulled back. It was at that moment I was shown how very, very little I knew about gryphons.

He sat beside me, tucking me under his wing, and pulled me half under his body. By some miracle, he managed not to crush me under his weight as he fluffed his feathers and settled half on top of me.

His beak carefully tucked my body beneath him, a stray arm here, and a leg there. He wasn't satisfied until my body was completely hidden under his feathery body.

Not sure if I should laugh or panic, I tried to connect with his mind, hoping to figure out what was going on inside his skull. I was met with crackling fuzz. Finally, a single word whispered through the bond.

Protect.

I sighed in frustration. It was much harder to connect with a beast than a man. So he wanted to protect me? For several long minutes, I lay motionless under my overly protective bird mate, trying to decide on my next move. Should I wait him out? At some point he had to shift back, right? Or should I politely ask him to move?

Deciding I didn't have the necessary patience for options number one or two, I squirmed. I wiggled around in the sand beneath him. It took far longer than I liked, and I was able to free an arm, and then a second arm. The beast released an annoyed screech and quickly tucked my freed limbs back beneath him.

Sugar honey iced tea! When I'd said I wanted a romantic walk down the beach with my mate, this wasn't what I had in mind. Okay, so it was cute in a protective sort of way.

Stop moving.

The word came through loud and clear through the mental link. Oh, now he wanted to talk?

"Get your fat butt off me!" I wheezed, fruitlessly pushing against his weight.

In response, he ruffled his feathers, completely unbothered by my outrage.

I wiggled some more, groaning as the gritty sand slid inside my shorts. To my disgust, my shirt rode up over my bra. Sand scraped against my back and worked its way under my bra strap. I groaned in annoyance. Nothing stuck with you more than damp sand in your butt-crack. It was possible I'd die of old age before I managed to get it out of all the places it wasn't supposed to be.

I blindly reached out my fingers, searching for anything I could use to help pull myself free. My fingers caught around something. Perhaps a root? I pulled on it, only to have the thing snap and whip across the sand toward me. It was a long thin branch that tapered to a point at the end.

One moment, Trevor was there, and the next, he was gone.

Confused, I pushed myself upright and looked toward

my gryphon. I still clutched the branch, and it trailed through the sand as I pulled my arm toward me.

The mythological beast wiggled his butt, preparing to attack. I screamed as he leaped toward me. His body sailed over me, wings softening his landing behind me. The massive gryphon didn't make a sound as he pounced on the end of the stick.

My mouth fell open in disbelief.

Trevor hadn't been lying! My quiet, elegant mate was playing with a stick like an overgrown kitten! I was used to behavior like this from Knox or Dagger, but not from Trevor. Never. The only other person less likely to chase a toy for fun would be Mace. I bit my tongue to keep from laughing at the mental image that thought summoned.

Still not believing what I was seeing, I drug the stick across the sand, its tapered tip tracing a line in the sand. Trevor hopped, his butt wiggling and tail twitching. Leaping across the sand, he chased the stick. I couldn't help it; I burst into delighted laughter. I'd always wanted a pet, and this had to be the best kind.

Hopping to my feet, I ran down the quiet beach. Behind me, the overgrown bird-kitty chased after me, batting at the stick with his golden talons. Birds squawked, and their feathers flashed as they darted away from us.

I ran toward the water, bursting into giggles when I glanced over my shoulder to find Trevor pacing just out of the water's reach. His feathery ears were pinned back, and his tail swished in annoyance.

"Water isn't your thing, huh?" I shouted.

Water gross. Bad mate. Come back.

Our mental bond was growing stronger. "And sitting on me was you being a good mate?" I raced back up the beach.

Yes. Keep mate safe. Trevor followed, hot on my heels. He could have easily overtaken me, but he played along, letting me think I was getting away before he'd flap his wings and race after me.

From the corner of my eye, I caught sight of the brilliant, orange-painted villa. The rest of my mates were still sleeping in the woven hammocks. An idea came to me, and I couldn't hold back my laughter.

Turning, I ran straight toward the middle of the courtyard with the nearly elephant-sized gryphon thundering across the sand behind me. I drug the stick through the sand, whipping it back and forth as though teasing a house cat.

What could possibly go wrong?

6

XERXES

I watched through slitted eyelids as Ryls ran toward us, her eyes sparkling with mischief. Her cheeks, which had been far too pale lately, were rosy from exertion and laughter.

For a perfect moment, she looked carefree. This was what I wanted for her all the time. It tore at my heart to see her sad, with dark smudges of fatigue under her eyes. She'd tried to hide it and worked to keep a smile on her face, but I could see the weariness in the tired slump of her shoulders.

Midnight and Ridgeforce's powerful hold over the world frightened her, and she'd taken it upon herself to wipe them from the face of the earth. It was the type of decision the jaguars could make without missing even a minute of sleep, but for Ryls, taking lives—even evil ones— weighed heavy on her conscience. We only had a few days here before we needed to make our next move, but I was determined to make sure she enjoyed every minute of it.

And that's why I remained motionless as the wicked

little vixen enthusiastically led a monster-sized gryphon toward us. I braced myself and hoped Trevor was in control of his beast, otherwise, this was going to be messy.

Ryls streaked past us, cackling like a banshee over her prank. The hammocks rocked wildly as all the trees in the courtyard shook from the weight of the rampaging gryphon.

The beast's large shoulder rammed into the side of Knox's hammock, flipping him unceremoniously onto the ground. Before Knox had time to react, Trevor collided with both Mace and Jett's hammocks, dumping them onto the ground with simultaneous thuds.

I was spared a similar fate, but still had the wind knocked out of me when Trevor's tail whipped in my direction and slapped me in the chest. The commotion roused Anzac, and he sat bolt upright... just in time to be knocked out cold by a wildly flapping wing. I had to hand it to the jaguars; other than Anzac, the others were quick to react. They sprang to their feet and rushed after the trouble-making pair.

I realized too late they'd misunderstood Ryls's happy squeals of laughter. They thought she was shrieking in fear, probably due to the freakishly large, mythological creature stalking after her.

Sighing over my lost nap but unwilling to miss the next part of this chaotic adventure, I rolled from the hammock to my feet and blurred after them. Not particularly eager to be trampled or bruised, I was careful to stay out of the way of the stampede.

The jaguars yelled threats, trying to distract the gryphon from what they believed was his prey—their mate. However, his prey was a stick, not the sassy female who was doing her best to give her jaguar mates gray hair and chest pains.

Mace caught up with Trevor first and grabbed his tail, hoping to slow the galloping beast. Gryphons were known to be peaceful creatures, but they have two places on their bodies that anyone with a desire to live shouldn't touch.

First, never grab their tails. Second, only their mate can touch their wings and live to talk about it.

Trevor turned toward Mace. I awoke my power to make sure it was ready if I had to react quickly and intervene. The gryphon shrieked a warning that had every warm-blooded creature on the island trembling in terror. Except for me... and Ryls.

I was stunned speechless when Trevor turned and continued the chase without dismembering Mace. A few days before, he had confided to me that he still struggled to accept Ryls's other mates, but the simple fact that Mace was still breathing and had gotten nothing more than a warning screech was a sign that the beast had accepted Mace as family.

A smile spread across my face, and a heavy weight lifted off my chest. I'd been worried about my old friend adjusting to sharing his mate, especially after the trauma he'd gone through. But he was going to be just fine in our odd little family.

Ryls's laughter echoed as she took off faster down the

beach. She was moving so fast that sparks seemed to fly from her feet. I made a mental note to add that to the list of unexplainable impossible abilities our mate continued to throw at us.

The gryphon was delighted at the newly intensified game. I watched in awe as the gryphon, who was running on four legs, had to flap his wings in order to gain enough speed to keep up with Ryls.

She was so caught up in her game she seemed unaware of her shiny new ability. Finally realizing she was leaving him behind, Trevor released another hair-raising, ear-splitting shriek, confirming the jaguars' impression that he'd gone fully beast mode and was hunting the little redhead. He wasn't, but I doubted anyone could convince the jaguars of that now.

In perfect unison, and without missing a step, the jaguar shadow shifted into their cats. They pushed themselves hard to catch up to the pair, and I was shocked at the speed at which they began closing the distance between themselves and the gryphon. I'd been unaware of the true speed of jaguars, and seeing it in person was incredible.

Trevor thundered across the sand, hot on her heels. There was a steep drop-off at this end of the beach, and it was hard to spot until it was too late. If you fell off it, you'd likely break something, but you weren't likely to die. Ryls was running out of beach, but she wasn't slowing down.

For the first time since this game started, fear tightened my chest with its icy hand. If he didn't stop, he would run her over. There was no way she'd survive being crushed by the paranormal world's version of a tank. And knowing she'd regenerate didn't help. I don't think any of us would get used to watching the love of our mostly immortal lives die.

I prepared to teleport, hoping to snatch her away, but I wasn't going to be fast enough. Nor were the jaguars snapping at Trevor's back legs.

With a scream of delight, Ryls jumped off the embankment. Throwing herself into the air as though she wasn't bound by the laws of gravity holding the rest of the world captive. With a hard thrust of his wings, Trevor leaped into the air after her. The snap of his wings created a tornado of stinging sand that forced the jaguars to stop.

I watched, spellbound, as the power from the speed at which Ryls had been running made it appear her body was floating through the air, her legs moving as though she were still running as she tried to keep the momentum going as long as possible. It was a long jump that would have broken every world record and then some. Before she even had a chance to feel the pull of gravity, Trevor's golden talons wrapped around her middle and lifted her into the light blue sky.

On the beach, the jaguars growled. Pacing and snarling, they gazed up at the winged predator, anger in their glowing eyes. Sticking my hands in my pocket, I strolled down to the water's edge and stood among the angry kittens.

It took a minute, but one by one, they began to shift.

"Why aren't you doing something?" Knox roared. His

lips pulled back, revealing long sharpened canines. He was still partially shifted.

"Calm down. Trevor won't hurt her," I reassured the snarling shifters.

Pulling my phone from my pocket, I quickly tapped the screen to start recording and held it up toward the sky. Gryphons love spending time with their mate in the air. Before they'd been forced to hide from society, gryphons had been known for the elaborate aerial acrobats they performed with their fated mate. I was beyond curious to see how Trevor would adapt the dance for Ryls since she was a different species and, well, tiny.

Ryls had only flown once, and she'd refused to try again since that day. Believing she was going to lose her mates and seeing the death and destruction around her had left scars on her soft heart. Knowing she'd very nearly lost control and scorched Earth had left her with immense guilt. The trauma of Anzac dying had been more than she could take, and it had left her raw.

She was consumed with the need for revenge, but she'd also avoided almost anything to do with that day, rarely speaking about it. Her ability to fly seemed to be connected to those awful memories, and she'd change the subject when we brought it up. It was unfortunate, as it was an ability that could help keep her safe. There were few para-normals on Earth who could take to the sky.

I wanted Ryls to feel the joy and freedom that came with flying, and none of the fear that came with falling. It appeared the gryphon wanted something similar. Spiraling up into the sky, he suddenly opened his claw and released Amaryllis. She began to drop toward Earth at a dizzying speed.

"Calm down?" Knox's skin rippled, and his eyes glowed. "You want me to calm down while the insane monster up there toys with our mate? What if he kills her?"

"Trevor's not going to kill her. Gryphons aren't an aggressive species and would never kill their mate," I explained, trying to split my attention between Knox and the pair in the sky. "He's courting her."

I glanced down the beach and caught sight of Anzac jogging down the beach toward us. His face was a mask of rage and his muscles bunched, ready to attack. Too bad naptime hadn't improved his surly demeanor.

Shaking my head, I focused back on the sky. Trevor flattened his wings against his body and dove after the free-falling redhead.

"Courting is like dating?" Dagger was the one to speak up this time.

"Exactly." Nodding, I flicked the screen on my phone to zoom in, hoping to capture better footage.

"Couldn't he just take her to a restaurant or movie? Like a normal person?" Mace snarled.

"Yeah. None of us have had the chance to take Ryls on dates yet. Except for the dragon," Knox grumbled.

"There will be plenty of time for us to enjoy date nights with her." I couldn't wait for my words to be true.

Our battles on Earth were almost finished, and then maybe we'd have time to figure out the dynamics of our group. We didn't even know the basics yet. Where did we want to live? Did we want to spend our time traveling the world? Did she want to work? Or spend all her time being pampered and adored by her mates? Did she want kids? And if she did, how many?

Would it even be possible for us to have offspring? We knew a phoenix could have children with a human male, but could they have them with other paranormals?

Trevor's wings stretched out, gently brushing against Ryls as they plummeted toward Earth at a gut-wrenching speed. She was grinning wildly, without a trace of fear or concern marring her beautiful face.

Trevor closed the small gap between them, rubbing against her like an adoring cat. Reaching out, she buried her fingers in the dark feathers of his back. Once the gryphon made sure Ryls was pressed against his back, he began to angle away from the ground. I would have preferred he moved a little faster, but at least he hadn't waited until the last millisecond.

The ground eagerly rushed up to meet them, and Trevor pulled away from it, barely missing our heads. His massive body and imposing wingspan cast a dark shadow on the beach. Ryls perched on his back like a conquering warrior queen. Her head was thrown back in laughter, and her wavy hair whipped around in the wind as Trevor once again lifted her into the sky high above our tiny island.

He soared so high that they were little more than a dark speck in the baby blue sky. After circling overhead several times, Trevor plunged toward Earth a second time. This time, they plummeted toward the tropical waters of the ocean. Moments before they would've plunged into the sea, he banked, making a sharp turn and moving back up into the sky with a laughing Ryls still clinging to his back.

Being tossed around the sky must have given Ryls confidence, because a glow flickered to life from Trevor's back. When he tilted to the side, I caught sight of my mate stretched out on the gryphon's back. She'd shifted, showing off her fiery wings.

Her wingspan was impressive, but in comparison to the beast she was riding, they were almost comical. It was like a hummingbird resting on the back of a Golden Eagle.

As Trevor darted around the sky, Ryls would periodically flap her wings as if working up her courage to try flying again. It didn't take long.

It amused me to no end that whenever Ryls spoke about her life of being safe and avoiding adventures. She made herself sound like a mousey woman who was scared of the world, but from what I saw, she was a woman who met every new challenge head-on with an eager determination. Which is exactly what she did next.

Ryls pushed herself off his back.

"Why did she do that?" Knox was on the verge of a meltdown. "All she needed to do was hang on. You had one job, Ryls! One job!" he moaned, pulling at the roots of his hair in agitation.

"Come on, little bird. Spread those wings and fly," Jett murmured encouragement she was too far away to hear.

I smiled, glad she would hear him when she watched

the video. Jett was a quiet man, and I hadn't figured him out yet, but his encouragement of her had me respecting him more.

Ryls fluttered around Trevor, lurching hard to the left and then to the right as she worked to control her fiery wings. It didn't take long for her to get the hang of it. With gentle prods and nudges from Trevor, she was soon fluttering along, albeit slowly.

She stayed close to Trevor's side. He would occasionally turn his head to her, pride showing across his features, and I don't think the gryphon could have fallen any more in love with her. I was surprised at a flash of jealousy that shot through me over the time my old friend was sharing with our mate. I wanted it to be me spending time with her. The need to complete the bond was becoming a need stronger than my body's need to eat or sleep.

Shoving my jealousy to a dark corner of my mind, I watched as Ryls gained confidence. She began to ride the gusty currents around the island, dipping and soaring as though riding a rollercoaster.

The gryphon screeched, darting after her with glee. It was hard to believe this was Trevor—my quiet, reserved friend. He was acting like a teenager with Ryls. After everything he'd been through and experienced, it was incredible getting to see him frolicking with our mate. I don't think I'd ever frolicked in my life, but I suddenly had a burning desire to try it.

The jaguars finally relaxed, sitting down on the sand and leaning back to watch the show playing out above us.

Ryls tucked her wings against her body and dropped head-first toward Earth.

Trevor did the same, using his wings to control his fall so that he stayed just slightly behind Ryls. If she was unable to pull up fast enough, with a powerful thrust of his wings, he'd be able to snatch her back in time.

Ryls spun and twirled. Sparks flew from her fiery wings, creating an intricate swirl of light in her wake. It was breathtaking, and easy to forget she was falling out of the sky.

Mesmerized by her elegance, we were abruptly yanked from our trance when she disappeared in an explosion of feathers and dust. We stared, slack-jawed, as the debris drifted toward Earth like morbid confetti.

I was beauty,
I was grace.
Until a bird,
Smacked my face.

*F*rankly, it was a shocking turn of events for both of us. On the ground, humans never expect to have a bird collide with their face. Likewise, in the air, birds never expect to have a human collide with their face.

The swift, brutal impact was powerful, and it created a stunning aerial magic trick. With a poof, the bird exploded into a cloud of white feathers that fell like confetti toward the earth. With a slightly bigger poof, my limp body exploded into fire, sending a cloud of ash drifting toward my horrified mates.

At least that is how Trevor described the reactions of my mates who'd been watching from the ground. The impressively clear video Xerxes recorded on his cellphone, showing the fiery and feathered fatalities, filled in the remaining blanks in my memory. It had been impossible to recall anything after the bird crushed a portion of my skull and shoved bits of shattered bone into the important parts of my brain. Thankfully, my death was nearly instantaneous.

The part of the video I found particularly amusing was the part where my mates lost their crap as a gust of wind spread my ashes in a beautiful burial at sea.

When I'd exploded into a dramatic cloud of ash, the gryphon screamed and frantically clawed at the air, trying to gather my ashes. It was a task made a thousand times harder as his wings frantically flapped, helping the wind scatter the ashes across the sea. Meanwhile, on the ground, my jaguars and dragon mate waded into the sea to scoop some of my ash.

My magic always called the ashes back together. It became glaringly obvious as I watched the video of my mates panicking that I'd forgotten to inform them of that nifty fact. Oops. My bad.

While my magic had the ability to pull itself back together, it unfortunately didn't have the ability to bring me back in a more comfortable situation. I came back wherever the majority of my ashes were. Which is why I regenerated at the same time I crashed beneath the water's surface.

It was like when I had a nightmare and jerked awake, gasping for air and trying to figure out where you are. Except in this case, I'd died... and I was underwater. This would have been fine if I were a mermaid, but I was a phoenix.

Thankfully, the water was less than ten feet deep. With a couple of kicks, my head broke the surface. I gagged and coughed, trying to expel the water from my lungs and avoid drowning. Xerxes appeared at my side and wrapped his arms around me. Pulling me to shore, he continued squeezing me tight enough to wring the last of the water from my lungs.

I suppose that's what I got for showing off. Dying sucked. What didn't suck was the way all my men gathered around me, desperate to make sure I was okay. I hated the lines of worry on their faces, and knowing I'd caused them, but I loved the feel of their touch as they stroked my skin, reassuring them I was okay.

"I'm fine, I'm fine!" I waved them off and sat up.

The guys weren't having it, and neither was the gryphon. Trevor crashed to Earth, screeching in frustration. Or maybe it was panic? Or anger? I honestly had no idea. He galloped toward us, shifting to his human form at the last second and shoving through the guys to kneel beside me.

"I'm so sorry! I was focused on you and didn't notice the bird. I should have seen it. Why didn't I pay closer attention?" Trevor cupped my face, covering it in kisses.

"It's not your fault. It's not like you flung the bird into my face." I laughed, but Trevor didn't.

Resting his forehead against mine, Trevor's eyes closed, and he breathed in my scent.

"Trevor, seriously, it's no big deal." I took in the worried faces around me. "You guys have to get used to me dying, or you are going to be really stressed out. Plus, I'll always look like I'm in my twenties, and at this rate, y'all are going to end up with wrinkles and white hair."

Trevor leaned back and tenderly brushed his knuckles across my cheek. Guilt lurked in his eyes, and it broke my heart that our incredible playtime had turned into something upsetting for him.

Placing my hands on his face, I pulled him closer. "Listen to me. It happened way too fast. Stop beating yourself up! At least I came back. The poor bird didn't." I winced and sent a mental apology to the bird.

"I think it's time we get you home before you find something else to get into." Xerxes lifted me into his arms, and as the fabric of his shirt rubbed against my bare skin, I remembered I was naked and felt my cheeks heat.

As I looked at the sexy hunks around me, other things began to heat up as well. I could definitely think of some things I'd like to get into... or, more accurately, *into me.*

THERE WAS a serious downside to having mates with the ability to smell a scent half a mile away. It didn't take more than a few steps before all seven men caught the scent of my arousal and inhaled deeply.

The muscles in Xerxes's chest stiffened, but his stride

lengthened. The rest of the guys kept pace with him, watching me with hungry eyes. Other than Xerxes, they were all as naked as jaybirds. It gave me an incredible, unobstructed view of their magnificent bodies. Heat rushed to my penis flytrap as my eyes trailed across the impressive evidence of their arousal.

Jett gripped his length, giving me a wink.

My heart tripped over its own beat before fluttering around like a blind bat inside my chest.

"Sounds like you have an arrhythmia, Koala Bear. Some people die from that. You should get it checked," Anzac teased. He didn't break eye contact as his hand stroked his stiff erection.

"I wouldn't mind," I whispered, trying to wipe any drool from the corner of my mouth discreetly.

"I want to know if it is possible for you to die from too many orgasms," Mace wondered out loud.

"Sign me up for that study!" The men laughed at my enthusiasm, but I didn't care at this point.

"She died once during sex with Knox and me. It scared us to death." Dagger laughed.

"Yeah, but that was from the brain bleed she didn't know was happening after she fell in the bathroom. Dying from back-to-back orgasms would be completely different." Knox grinned at me and flicked his partially shifted and longer tongue at me.

Chills slid down my skin at the reminder of the things the long, roughened jaguar tongues could do. The ache between my legs was growing more demand-

73

ing, and I tried to slip a hand between my thighs to ease it.

"Let me help." Xerxes's rough voice was pitched low, causing my body to hum like a tuning fork. He shifted me in his arms so that my legs wrapped around his torso as he kept moving.

"How? Ohhh!" My eyes crossed, and my legs trembled as I clung to him.

Xerxes wrapped his arms under my butt. One arm provided a makeshift seat to keep me from falling. With his second hand free, he'd managed to find my slick entrance and had slid a finger inside me. Xerxes did all this without breaking stride, and the steady rocking as he walked was providing incredible friction against my clit.

Uncrossing my eyes with Xerxes's finger stroking me was impossible, so I gave up and closed my eyelids.

"Open your eyes, Ryls," Dagger purred.

Blinking hard, I tried to bring him into focus over Xerxes' shoulder.

"Yes. Look at them. Let them watch as I pleasure you," Xerxes ordered.

It was too much, and I bit down on my hand to stifle my scream as I came apart, giving myself over to my release. I clung to him, my breath coming in short pants.

"That's my good girl," he praised, a finger still flicking lazily inside me. "Let them enjoy this teaser, because they don't get to watch the rest."

8

RYLS

We'd reached the villa, and Xerxes blurred inside and straight to the bedroom. He kicked the door closed. Freeing his hand, he reached down and locked it. I watched as his magic crackled on the doorknob.

"What did you do?" I studied the door curiously.

Xerxes gave a low chuckle. "Party trick."

My question was answered when the knob rattled, and Anzac cursed. "Drakon! Call back your magic and open this door."

Xerxes lowered me onto the bed, a wicked tilt to his lips that caused my entire body to quiver in anticipation.

"Drakon!" Dagger had joined Anzac at the door.

"I'm a patient man, but that patience is gone. I'm about to bond with my mate, so I suggest you all go away before I snap your necks." Xerxes hadn't raised his voice, but it carried through the room as though he'd bellowed each word.

"You're joking, aren't you?" I fumbled with the buttons of his shirt. Even on an island, the crazy man wore a dress shirt.

"I've waited long enough for this, to claim your body—inside and out. I will kill anyone who interrupts us," he stated matter-of-factly, catching my lips in a kiss.

Panic shot through me. What if the jaguars didn't take no for an answer? They didn't like taking orders.

"Stop worrying, my queen. They already moved out into the courtyard. Only an idiot would challenge a dragon claiming his mate." Xerxes's lips traveled down my throat to my breasts.

I arched my back, begging to feel his lips and touch on the sensitive skin. Xerxes didn't have to be asked twice. His mouth closed around part of my left breast, and his tongue teased my nipple into a hard peak. Not wanting my right breast to be neglected, he gently massaged it, his thumb brushing against the tender nipple.

My fingers continued to work at the buttons on his shirt, but I was finding it hard to concentrate. Frustrated and impatient, I did the logical thing and set his shirt on fire. The flames hungrily devoured the shirt but didn't touch his skin.

"Did you just burn my shirt?" he asked, trailing kisses back up my neck to my mouth.

"Mmm-hmm," I hummed. "It was in my way."

A rumble of amusement came from Xerxes. "Such a naughty girl."

"You can buy another. Better yet, just go shirtless." I bit his full bottom lip.

Ignoring my protests, he pulled away and unbuckled his pants. "These are my favorite pants. I prefer you not turn them to ash."

Scooting back, I leaned against the headboard and watched the strip show. I opened my mouth to give a saucy retort, but nothing came out, and my mouth refused to close as his pants dropped. Xerxes was manly perfection.

He raised a brow. "See something you like?"

I nodded my head enthusiastically while my mouth decided it was time to drop something witty. "Yes, your face. I like it."

What. Was. Wrong. With. Me?

Confusion crossed his face. "I'm glad?"

To my horror, my mouth wasn't finished humiliating me. "You're so hot, I'd like to bake cookies on you."

Xerxes began crawling up the bed toward me, his bottom lip caught between his teeth as he fought back laughter. There was a flash of fang that had my temperature rising. "Oh, would you now?"

My attention was drawn to his erection, and my brain glitched. "I usually have to sign for packages that big."

I slapped my hand over my mouth, keeping it from blurting anything else that would embarrass me. What would it blurt out next?

Maybe, 'I'm not into watching sunsets, but I'd love to see you go down?'

Or possibly, 'You're like my pinky toe, because I'm going to bang you on every piece of furniture in this house?'

Or how about, 'Are you a sprinkler? Because you're making me all wet?'

I love the way your mind works. Xerxes couldn't hide the amusement from his tone.

He'd been listening to my thoughts? Maybe he hadn't heard everything...

I heard everything. Xerxes's words brushed my mind. *And I'd love to go down and taste you.*

Moving between my legs, he gently pressed my knees apart. I was on display for him, and he drank in the sight, his breath growing ragged. Lowering himself, his tongue flicked out and traced my parted slit.

I whimpered, needing more from him.

Xerxes's tongue teased my entrance before delving inside. My body responded to his assault by sending a fresh wave of slick to coat my walls. Xerxes's tongue eagerly tried to lap up every last drop.

More, Xerxes growled. His eyes lifted to mine, and I gasped.

Gone were Xerxes's familiar human eyes. It was the dragon who watched me through slitted pupils. His tongue flicked against my g-spot. My body responded immediately and gave him what he wanted.

Xerxes kept his gaze locked on me as he roughly devoured his prize. My eyes widened as his tongue somehow thrust deeper, licking places that had never been licked before. Tongues weren't that long, or that thick.

You've never been with a dragon. We've developed a few tricks to please our mates, Xerxes explained through the link.

He brought me to the edge of my release, and then his tongue disappeared. I was left feeling empty and frustrated. Xerxes didn't waste time, though. Grabbing my legs, he yanked me flat on my back beneath him. With one hard thrust, he sheathed himself in my silky heat. I moaned, my hands exploring every inch of his bare skin within reach.

Xerxes set a steady, unhurried pace. His body moved sensually against me, undulating in a way that caused him to hit every spot both as he pulled out and thrust in. It was different from anything I'd experienced, but I was absolutely there for it.

"I searched for you for so long." He buried himself deep. "And now you're mine."

"Yes. Yours," I panted, dizzy from the intense pleasure and barely able to speak.

Xerxes nuzzled my neck. "I want to claim you."

He buried himself deep, his chest rumbling.

"Yes. Claim me, Xerxes. Make me yours." I tilted my head to the side, giving him better access to my neck.

"No, not there." He caught my lips, teasing my mouth. "Dragons claim their mates with a kiss."

"A kiss? You've kissed me too many times to count. Does that mean you already claimed me?"

His tongue slid across my bottom lip. "No, I haven't claimed you. This kiss is different."

Do it. Claim me, I whispered in his mind.

Xerxes's mouth pressed against mine, creating a seal. He breathed into my mouth, his spicy taste on my tongue was erotic. My throat burned, and my blood heated. Hotter and hotter. I started to pull away.

I'm giving you the kiss of fire. Branding you as mine.

My skin began to burn, and tiny flames licked down my skin. It quickly spread across Xerxes' skin, covering us both in fire.

There was a pop, and fiery confetti fell around us. The touch of my fire on his skin had branded him with my own mark. He was mine.

My claim activated something inside Xerxes. His body vibrated, and his kiss grew hotter until I felt like I'd swallowed the sun. There was a click in my chest, and power swelled, ebbing and flowing like a living, breathing thing.

There was another change. Xerxes pulled back his hips, slipping his erection from me. Releasing my lips, he growled my name. I glanced down at his fire-covered body, and my mouth went dry. What in the great Gatsby's ghost had happened to his manhood?

A line of hard ridges ran from just under the tip down to the base. The base had changed too. It had widened and was covered in a scaly texture. The biggest change, though, had to be the small tongue-shaped appendage that protruded in from the base. My mind was still trying to understand what I was seeing when Xerxes pushed his monster manhood back inside me.

The hard line of ridges felt amazing, but what had my

eyes rolling back into my head was the way the tongue-like protrusion stroked against my g-spot as though it had been created for that very purpose.

"Xerxes. What? How?" I moaned in bliss.

I took a minute for Xerxes to answer. "Dragons are part of the reptile family, and like many other reptiles, we once had hemipenes, or two penises. It is one of the things that our dragons' magic has adapted over the years to please our mates. Dragons discovered having a smaller second penis gives us the ability to stimulate as many erogenous zones as possible. We are only able to shift like this for our bonded mates."

My hands ran down his chest, needing to touch him, needing more of him.

Xerxes forced himself deeper until the base of his rigid erection was pressed hard against me. Just when I thought things couldn't get more amazing, Xerxes ground his hips against mine, the textured scales at the base of his erection creating mind-boggling friction against my clit.

My body shuddered in response to the overwhelming sensations bursting inside me like a thousand tiny explosions. Xerxes's control began to slip, and his eyes glowed. With a growl, he became rougher, driving us faster and faster toward our release.

All I could feel was heat, fire, and pleasure.

"Come for me, beautiful mate," Xerxes growled into my mouth.

My body obeyed, and my orgasm slammed into me.

Xerxes's body shook as he found his own release. We collapsed on the bed in a satisfied, sweaty heap.

"You're so hot, you've turned this room into a sauna," the dragon rumbled into the mattress.

I blinked through the haze of bliss, and my eyes widened. "Xerxes? The bed is on fire!"

9

ℛℒ8

*W*alking out of the bathroom, I worked a comb through my freshly washed hair. Xerxes was sitting on the end of the much smaller guest room bed. The bed in the master bedroom had burned to ash before we got the fire out. Xerxes was smug, proud that he'd caused me to lose control of my fire.

I could still hear the guys working to clean up the mess in the bedroom. They'd refused my help, telling me to take a shower and rest.

Xerxes was staring at his phone, forehead creased and lips pursed.

"Is everything okay, X?" I kissed his cheek, breathing in his spicy scent. The sweet, burning cherry wood, spicy cinnamon, and velvet musk had me longing to rub against him and coat myself in his alluring fragrance.

"Yes." He sighed, and for a long moment, he continued to stare in bewilderment at the dark phone screen. "I think."

"Hm. You don't sound too sure about that." I ran my

fingers through his dark hair, trying to tease him out of the strange mood.

Xerxes tossed his phone on the cheerful yellow polka-dotted quilt. Reaching out, he pulled me onto his lap. Before I could react, he covered my neck and face in kisses. I struggled to get away, but secretly loved it.

He flopped back on the bed, hauling me down beside him. I snuggled close and ran a hand down his chest. He was worried and trying to distract me.

"Something is bothering you. Tell me." I laced my fingers with his and waited.

"My pilot called. He said Jackson asked him to return to the mainland to get him. Apparently, Jackson wants the pilot to bring him here, to the island. I tried to call Jackson, but there hasn't been an answer. It's unlike my cousin to change a plan without my approval."

My happy mood vanished faster than a toupee in a tornado.

"Hey. Don't worry." Xerxes stroked my cheek. "I'm sure it is fine. Jackson is probably just trying not to bother me with every detail."

Anxiety tightened my chest, and my stomach twisted. It wasn't okay, and we both knew it. Jackson must have terrible news if he wanted to tell Xerxes in person... and interrupt what was supposed to be an impromptu honeymoon with my mates.

Curling tighter against him, I chewed on my lower lip and tried to think clearly. Panicking wouldn't help anyone. "When will he arrive?"

Xerxes slid his arm under me and rested his chin against my head. "The pilot left almost immediately after dropping us off. I hadn't noticed his call until we got back from the beach. He will land and pick up Jackson up within the hour. Once he refuels, he will head straight back here."

The next few hours were going to be stressful as we waited to find out whatever news Jackson had for us. I closed my eyes, suddenly feeling exhausted.

I PACED on the edge of the tiny airstrip, watching the skies for any signs of the plane.

"Ryls, come sit down. You're making me anxious, and the last thing we need is for you to burn the island down." Knox tried to joke, but it fell flat. There was no missing the tight lines of worry around his eyes.

We were all stressed. Xerxes had considered contacting his third in command, but that would alert more people to our current location. We hoped to avoid that. Besides, for all we knew, Jackson was just coming to surprise us.

I didn't believe that for a minute. I blew out the breath I hadn't realized I was holding. Whatever he wanted to talk about was bad news.

Xerxes's head snapped to the horizon, and the rest of my men quickly did the same. His voice was low when he announced, "The plane is nearly here."

Crossing my arms under my breasts, I shifted my

weight from foot to foot as I watched the tiny black speck turn into a plane. The pilot landed smoothly, and it hadn't even come to a complete stop before we were running toward the plane.

The plane's door flew open and crashed hard against the side of the plane. Time slowed as my brain struggled to comprehend the scene playing out in front of me.

The pilot's body toppled down the stairs like a human slinky. Vomit rose in my throat. Human bodies didn't move like that. He hit the ground, his neck twisted at an inhuman angle. Dark blood spread out in a pool around him, and his unseeing eyes stared back at us. He was dead.

I staggered, falling to my knees on the searing hot concrete of the runway. I'd only met him once, but he didn't deserve to die. Especially not like this. It was cruel.

Mace and Anzac rushed forward toward the dead pilot, but stopped cold at the soft click of a gun cocking.

"That's close enough, boys." An unfamiliar man's voice came from the shadowed cabin of the plane. "Take a step back, or Jackson will meet the same fate as the pilot."

I let out a cry when Jackson stepped out of the shadow. There was a gun pressed to his temple, and dark bruises covered his handsome face. Jackson's hands were cuffed, and his eyes were unfocused.

Xerxes, can you talk to him through your mental link? My brain was still struggling to make sense of what was happening.

No. There's a wall blocking our telepathic communication, Xerxes growled in frustration.

I decided to try to connect with Jackson's mind, but hit the same impenetrable wall. Realization dawned on me. Memories of my time held captive in the facility flashed through my mind. One ugly scene after another. One death after another. My body trembled. *They've drugged him, Xerxes.*

"Set down your guns. You have until the count of three," the man ordered. He stepped from the shadows, pressing the gun harder into Jackson's skin.

A long scar ran along the left side of his face from hair-line to chin. The skin was an angry violet-red color, and was a stark contrast to the sheet-white pallor of his skin. He was balding, but rather than accepting it, he was trying to rock a comb-over. With his hand not holding the gun, he pulled out a cigarette, and someone inside the plane lit it for him.

We hesitated, but when the man's finger twitched on the trigger, my mates lowered their guns to the ground. The guns would have made the fight easier, but if these men were human, the odds were still in our favor.

"Good. Now kick them away. And it better be a hard kick, or your friend here will have a bullet through his brain. I know how fast you shifters move, and I want those guns well out of your reach." The guy's sharp eyes watched as my mates followed his orders.

"How did you find him?" Xerxes demanded in a voice cold enough to freeze hell.

Gone was my thoughtful mate, and in his place stood the Drakon. Unbridled fury pulsed from him. If Xerxes flashed to the man's side, maybe he could snap his neck.

There had to be something we could do. A bead of sweat trickled down Xerxes's face, and the veins in his neck bulged.

The man holding a gun to Jackson's head laughed. "You can't pull any of your tricks on me, can you, Drakon?"

My mind reeled. What species was this man? From the little bit the guys had told me about other paranormals, none of the species were impervious to the Drakon shifters' abilities. This had to be a nightmare, and I'd wake up any minute.

"You can keep trying until your brain explodes, but your nasty little tricks won't work on my men or me." The man shoved Jackson forward.

"What are you?" Anzacs snarled.

"Me?" Scar-face took a long drag on his cigarette. "I'm human. Just an upgraded version."

"Impossible!" Xerxes roared.

Scar-face took his time responding. "Yes, it was impossible. Until Ridgeforce's brilliant scientists made a groundbreaking discovery right before your little slut destroyed their lab. It's such a shame that so much of the research was lost. All those years of testing gone to waste."

His eyes locked on me, and he clicked his tongue. "You should feel bad about that, Phoenix. Thanks to your impulsive decision, all that suffering and pain was for nothing."

"Don't talk to her." Trevor stepped in front of me. His chocolate wings snapped out, blocking me from Scar-face's view.

88

"Why do you think the government has been funding these experiments?" The evil man goaded us.

We remained silent.

"To make humans powerful enough to take down a paranormal. It isn't fair that humans are constantly unevenly matched in a battle with you freaks." Scar-face let out a long puff of smoke.

"That's ridiculous," Dagger protested. "Shifters are careful not to use their powers against humans. Heck! Very few humans on Earth even know paranormals exist."

"Oh, that's rich coming from you of all people!" The man laughed, the sound crawling over my skin like a thousand spiders. "Your shadow's body count is in the thousands, but you're going to stand here and act like you aren't a risk to humans? What kind of idiot do you take me for?"

My eyes widened, and I glanced at the jaguars from the corner of my eye. Thousands? Had they really killed that many people?

"We don't kill innocents." Jett's voice was cold and flat. "Everyone who died by our hand deserved it. Most deserved a far less merciful death than we gave them. Humans kill other humans far more frequently than a paranormal kills a human."

Scar-face waved his cigarette at Jett. "Sure. Keep telling yourself whatever you have to in order to sleep at night. Who made your shadow judge, jury, and executioner over whether humans should live or die?"

"Your government. That's who trained us!" Mace shouted.

"Yeah? Well, maybe your shadow was just a little too efficient. Perhaps you're the reason they decided humans needed a backup plan. Enhanced humans." He jerked the gun he was holding against Jackson's temple.

"Or maybe humans got greedy and wanted abilities they weren't born with. Abilities they weren't meant to possess." Trevor spat the words, his lip curling in disgust.

Scar-face shrugged and met Trevor's furious gaze. "I should thank you. It was your blood samples that really moved the research along. The entire formula is built on your DNA."

Even from my vantage point behind Trevor's back, I knew the man's words had hit their mark. Trevor clenched his fists, and his back muscles trembled.

"The docs in the lab spent decades trying to figure out how to activate the shifter DNA in your blood. No matter what they tried, they couldn't find the key to activate, or turn on, the parts of the DNA that controlled the shifters' abilities. At least not until they captured the Phoenix. Her blood had the missing spice that brought everything together. It shocked everyone when mixing her blood with the other samples instantly activated the shifter DNA. That discovery moved up the research time by several decades." Scar-face blew a smoke ring in my direction, and I wrapped my arms tighter around my middle.

"I don't understand. If the government wanted her blood, why didn't they just take it years ago? They knew where she was living while growing up."

The man shrugged. "It's the government, man. Half the

time, the left hand doesn't know what the right hand is doing. Plus, there were miles of red tape and piles of forms to fill out."

Scar-face leaned against the rail, his gun never leaving Jackson's head. "To add to the confusion, each group of scientists had different facets of the Phoenix's development that they wished to study. Some wanted her to grow up as a human, to more accurately test what instincts would come to her naturally. Whether being raised with humans, with no idea exactly what she was, would make her less of a ticking time bomb. Nature versus nature crap."

My mind felt numb, and I started shivering. After my mother's death, I'd been nothing more than a science experiment to the government and their scientists. Had I ever been seen as a living being? A person with feelings, hopes, and dreams?

The truth was ugly and stabbed like a knife through my heart. I had fewer rights or respect than a lab rat. Even if I shut down Midnight and Ridgeforce, I wouldn't be free. Not with the knowledge that my own government had its hand in this mess, too.

"The whole unstable Phoenix storyline has kind of given you a bad rap. But you are the last of her kind, so some of the scientists want to try and save her species from extinction." Scar-face flicked his cigarette butt to the runway. "I don't know why the world is so stuck on saving everything these days. The way I see it, if a creature can't adapt and survive, it doesn't deserve to live."

"None of this explains why you can block our abilities," Mace interjected, his patience growing thin.

"Or how you found us." Xerxes took a step forward.

"I was getting to the good part." Scar-face whistled, and two soldiers came out of the plane, machine guns raised. They moved single file down the stairs and stood between us and the plane, prepared to take us out if we so much as moved.

Satisfied we wouldn't rush the plane, he continued. "There was another issue. They did take her blood, several times, but it was almost as boring as a human's blood. She obviously had some weird crap in her DNA, but it was barely functioning. But when she was captured, they compared the new samples to the old samples and made a fascinating discovery. Best they could figure out, bonding with a mate activated her DNA. Like twisting a light bulb into a light socket. That's when a lot more people decided she was more valuable alive. Now everyone is scrambling to either get their hands on her or to make sure a rival doesn't."

Finding my voice, I peeked around Trevor. "So, what exactly is your plan? How did you find us?"

"As to how we found you, we have eyes and ears every-where." His cruel eyes glittered with malice and something predatory as he stared at me. "Also, and you are going to love this part, it turns out those of us who were injected with the activated Phoenix blood are drawn to you. It's odd, and from what I hear, it's almost like…" He tapped his chin as though thinking of a comparison. Turning back to me, his tongue licked his lips. "Like the lab-created a mate bond. Isn't that incredible? One of the side effects happens to be this strange pull toward you. That is very helpful for locating our missing mate."

He was lying; he had to be. But if he was lying, why did I feel like they were familiar? I searched inside my mind and heart, trying to prove he was full of crap and making it all up. Sweat trickled down my spine. Something was there. It wasn't a strong pull to them like I had with my natural fated mates. This thing felt synthetic and odd, but it was still there.

I was going to be sick. Spinning around, I stumbled to the grass and wretched until my stomach was empty, but still, my stomach heaved. Hot tears leaked from my eyes and trailed down my cheeks.

This couldn't be happening. How many men had they injected with my blood? If they could track me, they'd hunt me for the rest of my life. I would never feel safe, and my true mates would always be in danger.

This morning it seemed my life was looking up. I'd been happy. I guess it was too much to ask because life seemed to take delight in handing me a fresh, steamy pile of crap to deal with.

*I*gnoring me heaving on the grass, Scar-face barked out a warning. "All right, everybody back up."

I staggered to my feet. The men backed up, creating a wall between the soldiers and me. Trevor spread his wings in front of me, wanting to give me as much protection as possible, which was frustrating because I was the one who could die and come back, not him.

"If any of you so much as twitch, I'll shoot him. I'm far faster than a normal human, which means you can kill me, but you can't kill me fast enough to stop me before I pull the trigger."

Shoving Jackson forward, Scar-face followed him down the stairs. Eight soldiers dressed in black tactical gear and carrying machine guns followed him out of the plane.

They're all immune to my abilities, Xerxes whispered in my mind.

"Phoenix. Come here!" Scar-face, clearly the commander of this group, shouted.

I couldn't think of something I'd like to do less. It didn't matter, since Trevor refused to step out of my way.

"You better be standing in front of me by the count of five, or I will blow his brains out," he called.

It was a stupid threat. Jackson was the only thing keeping him alive. If Jackson died, these humans would be ripped to ribbons. At least that is what I believed until another soldier roughly pushed a second prisoner through the plane door and down the tiny metal stairs.

"Lee," I breathed my friend and guardian's name, stepping around Trevor.

"I knew you'd be happy to see him. We figured you'd want to bring your whole crew along on this adventure." A victorious smirk curved the commander's lips.

I clenched my teeth, fighting the urge to do something stupid since that was my calling card. Given a hard push, Lee tumbled down the stairs, falling to his knees. There was a sickening crack as something in his ankle broke. Lee grimaced, and agony twisted his features, but he bit back his scream, refusing to show weakness.

I focused my wrath on the guard who'd shoved my friend, and my eyes widened. I knew him. It was a face I never expected to see again.

Willard.

His blonde hair was cut far shorter than it had been when I'd known him as my guard. He was thinner than the last time

I saw him, but his muscles still bulged against the confines of his shirt and bullet-proof vest. His chocolate brown eyes lit-up when they landed on me, but the light quickly disappeared, and Willard grimaced as though he were in pain. That caused a pain to flash through me, which made absolutely no sense.

The commander followed my gaze to see what had captured my attention. "Do you remember Willard? Or should I reintroduce you guys?" the commander joked.

I said nothing, too afraid that if I opened my mouth, I'd lose control, and this whole situation would go downhill in a hurry.

"That's not a very nice way to greet one of your chemically bonded mates. Funny story about that." Scar-face grinned, showing his yellow-stained teeth. "It was a freak accident! Willie tried to save the blood samples and the vials of the lab-created cocktail before you blew the lab to hell. There was a lot of jostling as all the staff and soldiers tried to escape, and there was an unfortunate mishap."

Willard had stepped up beside the commander, and the commander slapped him on the shoulder. "Your boy was pretty cut up after the explosion knocked him and the tubes holding the vials of blood through a few walls. It was a nasty mess, and he wasn't supposed to survive. He had a miraculous recovery, although he's still picking glass out of his skin."

This was terrifying. I couldn't think, breathe, or move. I wasn't even sure if my heart was still beating. This could be happening.

Please let him be lying! My anguished scream echoed around my skull.

I stared at Willard. He wasn't the same man who'd guarded me during my involuntary stay at the lab. There was a new hardness to his face, like he was wearing an emotionless mask. His face while guarding me hadn't been necessarily kind, it had been indifferent. He'd never been cruel, though.

As my captor, he'd still treated me decently and allowed me to keep my tattered dignity. Never would I have expected him to turn to violence, and for some absurd reason, I felt hurt by his joining the dark side. I expected more from him, and it made absolutely no sense. How could you expect more from someone you didn't really know?

"All right, enough chatting. We're all going to walk up this beach nice and easy. No sudden movements?" The commander waited for us to agree, but was met with only silence.

"You are going to let my men cuff you one at a time. Any quick movements will send a bullet into Jackson's brain. Got that?"

The jaguars snorted. Cuffs made zero difference to a paranormal who could snap them like a piece of string. Slowly and obediently, each of my mates held up their hands, and I followed suit. The soldiers cautiously stepped in front of the guys, slapping the silver bracelets on their wrists with a sharp snap.

Willard switched places with another guard and strode

to me. As he leaned forward to put on the cuffs around my wrists, I recoiled from him. I couldn't get away, though, not unless I was willing to risk Scar-face shooting Jackson.

Willard breathed in deeply, taking my scent into his lungs. His lips brushed up my neck to press against my ear. The rough stubble of his jaw rubbed my skin.

Only the guns pressed to Lee and Jackson's heads kept me motionless.

His hot breath blew against my ear. "I need you to not do anything crazy."

A flash of annoyance shot through me. Why did everyone think I was liable to do something crazy if given the opportunity? I could behave and act like an adult.

Sometimes.

Fine, based on my recent track record, I probably shouldn't be left unsupervised.

"I need you to trust me," Willard whispered.

I snorted.

Willard made a quiet sound of frustration and tried again. "Listen to me, Amaryllis. I don't want you or your mates to get hurt. Play along until I can explain what is going on."

I worked hard to keep my face from revealing my surprise, or my confusion. What was Willard playing at? Was he just trying to keep me under control until they got me under lock and key? What if he was telling the truth? Would he actually help us?

I needed more information before I could make any decisions. First, I needed to know what Scar-face planned to do next. For now, playing along with Willard's request worked with my own plan. But should an opportunity present itself to get my mates out of this mess, I wouldn't pass it up on anything other than the word of my one-time jailer.

As soon as we had the cuffs on, the commander gave a sharp jerk of his head. The soldier to his right pulled a tiny remote from his pocket and clicked on it. There was a sharp prick of pain in my wrists. My mates must have felt the same thing because they cursed, yanking at the cuffs.

It was too late, though. The drug was already flowing through our veins at an alarming pace. As the poison spread, it took away my abilities, leaving me helpless. I was going to kick Willard so hard in the wrinkle berries that he'd choke on them. He wanted me to trust him? Well, we were off to a lousy start.

A tiny spark fell from my hand, and I froze, watching the ember fall to the ground. Commander Scar-face thought he'd leveled the playing field, but he'd made a serious error. They'd given me the dose the doctors were injecting me with during my stay at the facility, but I'd claimed two more mates since then, and with each of those mates, my power had increased.

My abilities were dulled, much like the buzz you might get from a glass of wine at dinner. But the effect wasn't going to last long. The inferno in my chest was already burning its way through the toxin in my bloodstream. Hope leaped in my chest, and Imp rubbed her wings together—which was super weird and extremely worrisome... for them, not me. I was finding I enjoyed her brand of crazy more and more.

This was the leg up I needed in the showdown that was brewing. For now, I'd play along. I allowed my eyelids to droop and began to drag my feet through the sand, but my mind was busy taking in everything around me.

I wasn't the nervous little Phoenix who'd longed for the adventure and who'd crashed into the Amazon. I'd trekked my way out of the Amazon, I'd survived torture at the hands of cruel doctors who treated me like I was a little more than an animal, and I'd lived through a battle that left several acres blackened. Heck! Less than twenty-four hours ago, I'd assassinated one the most powerful men in the world.

I was a freaking boss!

A tiny thrill of excitement, and something else, spread through my chest. It was dark and dangerous. It was the desire to hunt. I wanted to take these men out even if by taking people out, I also took myself out. Which shouldn't be a challenge since I took 'me' out all the time. I needed to let these soldiers take me to their home base, and then use my ability to die to take them all out in one fell swoop.

I had a talent for finding ways to die with my eyes closed and my hands tied behind my back.

As a wise man once said, I have a very particular set of skills...

It was almost time to put those skills into action.

11

DAGGER

hey settled us in on the patio outside the beach house, chaining each of us to one of the large trees surrounding the house. I guess they didn't want to risk us somehow working together and escaping.

I reached out in the mental bond, searching for Ryls or the rest of my shadow, but the link was quiet. The drugs in my system were making it impossible to concentrate or use my jaguar's abilities to communicate with each other or escape.

They brought a heavy metal chair into the middle of the courtyard. The guard named Willard eased her into the chair and quickly chained both her legs and her hands to the sturdy chair.

Pride warmed my chest. These men were scared of Ryls. Why else would you chain a woman who was barely five feet tall and couldn't even hold up her head due to the amount of drugs they dumped in her system? Her reputation had preceded her, and they knew to be very wary of her.

I was glad they were afraid, since that might deter them from getting too close to her. But I was also filled with fury over my inability to protect her. How had we been so stupid?

We'd gone to meet the plane fully armed just in case something was wrong. It didn't occur to us that Jackson might have been kidnapped and the plane hijacked. Even though we didn't have a crystal ball, I was swamped with the guilt that we should have seen what was coming and been better prepared.

Maybe if we had only sent two of us to meet the plane and the rest had hidden, we could have gotten the jump on them. Logically, I knew that was unlikely. The soldiers would have known exactly how many of us were on the island, and they would have threatened to gun down Lee and Jackson if the rest of us didn't show ourselves.

A short, balding soldier looped a second set of chains around Ryls's ankles and wrists. He was using it as an opportunity to brush his hand against her skin. I tried to growl a warning, but my throat and mouth wouldn't work. I'd been given a heavy dose of the tranquilizer and could barely keep my eyes open.

I watched the soldier, growing more agitated. What bothered me the most was how his body changed when he was near her. These men were acting like they could feel the pull of the mate bond. Even his breathing had changed when he was near her. He wasn't her mate, but his body was telling him differently.

How had this happened? I'd never heard of anything like this ever happening. Mates were given to us by fate. They definitely weren't created in a lab.

A migraine pounded away in my head as I tried to work through all the implications this new development might have. What would this mean for them? Was Ryls feeling a pull toward any of these men?

How many had been given her blood and could feel the pull? It didn't really matter, because they were all going to die. And as far as I was concerned, the sooner they died, the better. Unfortunately, I wasn't in a position to dish out death at the moment.

Anger continued to boil inside me like a volcano, ready to unleash its fury. This was supposed to have been a few days of carefree fun. A chance for us to finally spoil our precious mate. And what had she gotten? Half a day? How was that fair? She deserved everything that was wonderful in this life, but no matter how hard we tried, the world just kept dumping evil in her lap.

Testing my strength, I pulled on the chains, careful not to rattle them and draw the attention of the guards. I might as well have been human. The cuffs and chains didn't budge. Until this drug wore off, I was going to be severely limited on how much I could help.

The commander strolled through the glass patio doors, sipping from a water bottle that dripped with condensation in the tropical heat. He snapped his fingers, and one of the soldiers brought him a chair.

"Fancy meeting you here." He sat down and scooted the chair a few inches closer to Ryls, leaning toward her. "I'm Commander Hensel, and it is a pleasure to finally make your acquaintance."

I curled my lip in disgust. Was this buffoon really trying to flirt with her while he'd ordered her drugged and chained?

Ryls slurred a soft response that was barely audible, but it sounded an awful lot like she said, 'Go play in traffic.'

Hensel's hand shot out, slapping her across the cheek. I tried to jerk forward, but couldn't move. Ryls's head snapped to the side with a sickening crack.

My eyes burned, and my frustration brimmed over that Hensel's heart was still beating after he dared touch her like that. I desperately tried to access the mental link, but my mind was eerily silent. I was useless to my mate, and it wasn't something I'd ever forget or forgive myself for. I wanted to look away, but I didn't even have the strength for that.

As quick as he'd slapped her, Hensel reached out a second time and stroked along her jaw. He gently turned her to face him. "See what you made me do? There's no need to be rude. We're going to be working together for a very, very long time."

"If you're going to be two-faced, at least make one of them pretty," Ryls slurred, the words running together. She tried to spit at him but failed, and it dribbled down her chin.

Hensel gripped her jaw and chin hard enough to turn his fingers white. "I'm going to give you a pass this time, Phoenix. We'll blame the drugs for your lack of manners."

To my relief, Ryls said nothing. Her body remained relaxed even as his fingers bruised her face. They must have given her an insanely high dose of the tranqs if she was this relaxed. Ryls was a fighter with a wicked sense of humor, and the inability to stop herself from blurting out her every thought. She would have been fighting him tooth and nail if there were any strength in her body.

"You see, as a reward for capturing you, I've been appointed to a position overseeing the revamp of Project Phoenix Down. You'll be pleased to know our goals have changed some since the last time you spent time in a lab."

Releasing her face, he leaned back in his chair and crossed his arms. "Sure, there are still a few leaders who think you're too risky to be left alive, and they want to kill you. But after those recent successes of your blood activating the other shifters' blood, most of us realize keeping you alive opens the door to endless opportunities."

"Won't... stop," Ryls whispered, her words barely understandable.

"Don't be afraid. We know they won't stop coming for you. That's why we're not going to let that happen. We'll keep you alive," Hensel promised, a menacing grin stretching across his face.

He'd misunderstood her words. Ryls was trying to tell

him she wouldn't stop fighting them. She was warning him.

Hensel leaned back until his chair balanced on two legs. "I have to thank you, though. You and your men saved us quite a bit of work by assassinating Calvin. And right as we boarded the flight here, we got confirmation that Midnight's other two facilities had been leveled to the ground. Completely destroyed. Your team was thorough. They killed both directors, along with all their high-ranking staff."

Hensel gave a slow clap, and several of the soldiers joined in. "You guys are doing a fantastic job of cleaning house. There are only a few more people who need to go." He glanced at his watch. "And that'll all happen in about forty-eight hours, give or take a couple hours."

What was he talking about? By the sound of it, it was nothing good. I knew I should feel more upset about it, but I wouldn't shed any tears over Ryls's enemies being given a one-way ticket to hell. While I was suspicious about his motives and wanted Hensel dead, I wouldn't complain if her enemies turned on each other. I was all for anything that would reduce the number of threats to my mate's safety.

Hensel's phone rang, and he glanced at the caller's name. "Excuse me, sugar. I've been waiting for this call."

Leaning forward, he slid his thumb across Ryls's bottom lip. Rage pulsed through me, but vanished when I noticed a tiny movement I'd nearly missed. Ryls's hands had clenched at his touch.

The rest of her body remained relaxed and floppy, but I saw her fingers clench into a white-knuckled fist, and I could have sworn a tiny spark dropped from her left hand.

I blinked, trying to think past the drugs clouding my mind. Was Ryls truly out of it? Or was she playing possum? A new concern moved to the forefront of my mind. What if she was planning something? What if she tried to save us, and things went wrong?

The low murmur of the commander's voice drifted from inside the house. I strained to hear his conversation, but without my enhanced abilities, I couldn't make out the words. One of the guards walked by, gun at the ready, checking that none of us were trying to escape. He was the one Ryls had known. What was his name? Billy? No. It was something to do with being a penis. Willie? No, that still wasn't right. My brain throbbed as I tried to remember. Willard? Yes, that was it!

Willard was the one who shoved Lee down the stairs. And he'd been the guard who'd pressed his face to Ryls's neck. My chest rumbled with a low warning growl.

Willard glanced down at me, his eyes connecting with mine, and his mouth moved before quickly looking away. I could've sworn he whispered 'sorry,' but that made absolutely no sense.

What could he gain from apologizing? Did he hope saying sorry would save his useless hide? I snorted. Not a chance. The moment any of us got free, he was going to die. It was just a matter of which one of us got to him first.

After checking that the tranquilizers were still working

and the commander was still on the phone inside, Willard moved to take the empty seat in front of Ryls. He scooted forward on the seat until Ryls's knees were between his. Willard leaned in, his hand brushing up her neck. He turned her face to his, and I thought he was going to kiss her.

The taste of old pennies filled my mouth. I'd nearly bitten off my tongue in my rage. I spat the blood on the ground, but I could feel it trickling from the corner of my mouth.

He stopped just shy of his lips brushing against her plump bottom lip. Willard's lips moved, whispering something to her. Ryls's fingers dug into her palm, the only outward sign of her anger again.

Willard moved his face, brushing it along her cheek. His lips grazed her neck and moved to her ear. He brushed his hand through her tangled hair. This was the worst kind of torture I'd ever been forced to endure, and I found myself wishing Ryls would combust and take him out... even if it meant taking all of us out as well.

To my shock, Ryls's fingers relaxed, and her breathing calmed about halfway through the petting. I understood Willard had a fake chemical bond with her, but it shouldn't affect her. So why was his touch calming her instead of angering her? Then again, maybe I'd imagined the movements in her hands. It was possible that hallucinations might be a side effect of the drug.

"Getting a little impatient, aren't we? I told you guys we'd have plenty of time with our new mate once she is at the facility. We can work on figuring out what a mate bond means there. Besides, the scientists are eager to document our... interactions with her." He strode across the beautiful hand-painted tiles of the courtyard and jerked Willard away from Ryls.

I thought he'd be angry and maybe shove Willard. Better yet, maybe he'd punch Willard square in his face.

But Hensel threw an arm around Willard and slapped him on the back. "I know you waited a long time. You were forced to watch her, without being able to show your feelings. Don't worry. It'll be worth the wait. But first, let's get her back to the facility. This is not the time to get overly confident."

Yep, it was decided. Hensel would die first, and Willard would die next. How dare they treat my intelligent, hilarious, clumsy, adorable mate like she was little more than a booty call or a hunting trophy? My heart thudded harder from my rage, and pain shot through my skull. The ground tilted, and I had to fight to keep from passing out.

"The Senator told me our ride will be here tonight. We'll have promotions and a feast waiting for us. We just have to be patient, and you need to keep it in your pants for a few more hours."

Willard ran a hand through his short-cropped blonde hair and dropped his head in embarrassment. "Apologies, sir. She's so tempting."

Hensel chuckled, and his eyes scanned Ryls. "I get it. I definitely get it. All right, you guys go in the kitchen and see what this place has to eat. I'm starving."

Hensel settled back into the chair, a satisfied smirk on his face. "Ryls, you should have heard the Senator. He was thrilled at the news that you and your mates had been captured. I have a fat bonus check waiting for me as soon as we land. Everything is falling into place. Once the last few nay-sayers who think you need to be eliminated are out of the picture, we'll be in charge."

"How?" Ryls whispered.

The commander clasped his hands behind his head. "You want to know how we're taking them out? An emergency meeting has been called to discuss the fate of the Phoenix. They believe they're coming to a summit. They plan to present arguments on why the investors should cut their losses and get rid of you, and why it's too dangerous for any government to keep you captive to experiment on."

Hensel must be feeling awfully cocky about having captured us, to be so chatty about their plans. He believed we didn't have a chance in Hades of escaping. I hoped we'd get the chance to use this against him.

Hensel dropped his voice to a conspiratorial whisper. "What they don't know is that the train bringing them to the summit is going to have a tragic accident." He closed his fist before opening it and mouthing *boom*.

"Evil," Ryls slurred. "Innocents."

"Don't judge us. Some people will die, but you'll get to live." The commander stood and stretched his arms above his head. "Exciting stuff is about to go down, little girl. And you're going to get a front-row seat to the show."

Turning to a black-haired soldier with a buzz cut, the

commander barked, "Give them another dose. I want them out cold until we arrive in Switzerland."

"Yes, sir. On it, sir." The soldiers moved to follow his order.

Around me, Trevor, Xerxes, and the rest of my shadow struggled against their restraints. It was bad enough to watch helplessly as they interacted with Ryls, but to be knocked out completely was terrifying.

Willard appeared at Ryls's side, halting the soldier moving toward hers. "Except for the Phoenix. She's already so drunk she can't even talk, and I want her to know what's happening."

There was another sharp prick in my wrist, followed by a burning that traveled up my arm. I fought the drug, but my body finally succumbed to its effects. My eyes drifted closed, and the world turned black.

12

RYLS

My fingernails bit into the skin of my palms as I watched the soldiers inject more of the tranquilizer into my mates. I wanted to rip off these chains and turn the soldiers to ash.

I wanted to do something, but I couldn't. Not after the information Willard had given me. Like it or not, I had to bide my time and get the information that I needed.

Then I could get my revenge.

Willard thought our best shot was waiting until we were on the plane headed to the new facility that had been prepared for my arrival. He'd been told that the pilot wouldn't be given the coordinates until the plane was in the air. That meant we needed to wait to act until after they'd entered the new coordinates and knew where we were headed.

I hated to admit it, but Willard's plan sounded like it might work. It was still a huge gamble, though. One that I wished I could talk over with my mates. We were a team, and I hated knowing I was about to pull them into this without giving them a chance to provide input.

Espionage was not exactly my forte, as evidenced by the last twenty-four hours. I didn't really have a choice, though. If Willard was correct, there were twenty soldiers who'd been injected with the Frankenstein cocktail that included some of my blood. They all felt the pull toward me, which meant they could track me.

Some of those faux mates were here on the island; the rest would be at the facility awaiting my arrival. It was my best shot to take them out, otherwise, I might spend years always looking over my shoulder while they tried to slip between my sheets or kill me.

Willard had also given me a bit of hope. He had a connection who'd told him about a high-ranking politician who was open to hearing my side of the story.

I forced myself to remain relaxed, continuing my charade of being weak. All while praying I'd made the right choice when picking an ally.

DUSK HAD GIVEN way to an obsidian sky as the commander got news the plane had landed.

Two soldiers dragged me through sand toward the plane. The rough sand left abrasive wounds on my legs. It hurt like the worst carpet burn in history, but I focused on keeping my breathing slow and steady. I didn't want to

give the soldiers a reason to suspect I was completely
alert.

"Idiots!" At Willard's sharp tone, I peeked through
narrow slits in my eyes to see him stomping toward us.
"Are you two trying to waste time? She weighs nothing!
Dragging her is just slowing the boarding process. Get back
to the villa to help drag Mace. He's heavy as a grizzly, and
the guys are struggling with him. I'll take the Phoenix to the
plane myself."

The soldiers groaned, but apparently Willard out-ranked
them because the two guards dropped my arms like I was
on fire. I hit the sand like a sack of potatoes. Turned, they
headed back to the house without a backward glance.

"Sorry about that," Willard whispered, gathering me
into his arms.

"Whatever." I still didn't completely trust him, and I
wasn't exactly in the mood for conversation.

"The guys are being loaded now. Xerxes and Knox are
already on the plane; the others are behind us." Willard
ignored my rudeness. Although, to be honest, was it really
considered rude to not want to talk to one of the people
holding you hostage?

I stared at the stars twinkling in the sky overhead,
feeling my anger spreading like wildfire. It was consuming
everything inside me, leaving only fury in its wake.

I should have been enjoying dinner under the stars
with my handsome men in the villa's courtyard. We
should have been laughing over Knox's stupid jokes or
Jett's sharp wit. I should have been snuggling in Mace's

arms or kissing Xerxes. Imp should have been hopping around the firepit, scattering sparks to make Anzac and Mace jump.

Instead, my men were prisoners. All because of an insane desire for me to be dead or captured. If this is how all phoenixes were treated, it wasn't a shock that they tended to detonate and take out part of Earth with them. That option was looking better and better with each passing minute I wasn't allowed to be with my mates.

Willard's long strides carried me up a metal cargo loading door and into the belly of the dimly lit plane. Xerxes and Knox had been tossed onto the floor like garbage. A chain had been clamped to their cuffs, and then locked to a bolt in the floor. Even though the men were drugged and unconscious, these soldiers weren't taking any risks.

Walking past the men on the floor, Willard headed deeper into the plane. The front of the plane was divided from the cargo bay with a metal wall, and near that wall, there was a metal box. It was about the size of an airplane restroom, and I'd thought it was to store gear... right up until Willard opened the door to the box and shoved me inside.

"Sorry about this, Amaryllis. The commander ordered us to lock you in here, and if I disobey, it could blow my cover." Willard sounded genuinely apologetic, but I really wasn't in the mood for any more of his apologies, especially while he was locking the deadbolts on the door to my tiny metallic coffin.

PHOENIX REVENGE

"Stop talking, Willard." I dropped my forehead against the cool steel with a disgusted groan. "Please just go."

He paused, whispered a last *sorry*, then I heard his retreating footsteps. Now I had a new complication to figure out. My hope had been to be ready to attack when the plane landed at the undisclosed location, but unless I was a long-lost descendant of Houdini, that wasn't going to happen.

Boots pounded up and down the cargo door as my mates, Lee and Jackson, were all loaded onto the plane. The commander's booming voice echoed through the hold. "That's the last of them. Jose and Tom, you two strap-in back here to keep an eye on the prisoners. Everyone else, head around to the front and get ready for take-off."

Even though I was annoyed with Willard, I wished he'd been left in the back with us. I might need his help once we were in the air. Now I had to figure out an escape plan and execute it alone. Why hadn't I paid attention during my high school espionage classes? Oh, right! Because they taught me stuff like calculus instead of stuff I'd actually be able to use.

With a whine, the plane's engines came to life, the sound drowning out anything else. The walls of my metal prison vibrated from the powerful engines. I squeezed my eyes shut, not wanting to cry. Flying wasn't on my list of favorite activities lately, and doing it as a passenger inside a sardine can made it far less enjoyable.

My chest warmed, and Imp stretched her wings inside me. She was trying to reassure me I wasn't alone, and it helped to ease a little of the tight ache in my chest. I sagged against the wall as the plane picked up speed and lurched into the night sky.

Once in the air, I remained against the wall with my cheek pressed against the rough, rusted metal. This position also pressed my ear against the wall, and that's when I made a delightful discovery.

This wall must be against the main cabin's wall, because I could just make out the voices of the soldiers on the other side of the wall in the plane's passenger cabin. It was about as clear as using two paper cups and a string, but it was clear enough for me to understand most of what was being said in the front of the plane.

"I can't believe this mission went off without a hitch!" Soldier One declared.

Soldier Two scoffed. "I'm not surprised. The idiots sent after her on previous missions were morons. It was about time they sent us in."

"I expected the Phoenix to be more powerful. What a letdown. At least she's attractive," Soldier Three added.

The men laughed, and their ramblings droned on. I wanted to start trying to free myself, but I hoped to gain intel about our destination first. It was likely that my attempts to escape the box would be noticed, and the guards would raise the alarm.

I continued listening to the useless banter of the soldiers until I was bored silly. I'd reached the point of considering whether dying to escape boredom for a couple minutes was an option when the radio crackled to life.

The commander answered and relayed our current location. He was given coordinates, and the plane tilted to the side as the pilot adjusted our flight path. The commander updated the base with our ETA. We were an hour and fifteen minutes from the secret destination. It was time to get to work.

I pressed my palms against the metal seam of the door, wincing as the handcuffs dug into my sore wrists. Realizing the cuffs needed to go first, I focused on my magic and sent it surging into the unfashionable silver bracelets. Spider web cracks spread across the cuffs, and with a quick jerk of my hands, they snapped and fell to my lap. I repeated the process with the chains around my ankles.

Once free of my unwanted accessories, I again pulled on my magic and sent it rushing to my hands. The cold black metal slowly heated under the brilliant orange glow of my flattened palms.

The metal began to glow and slowly bend outward as it lost its integrity and became more pliable.

"Ready, Imp?" I whispered.

My chest warmed. Imp fluttered and sparked in my mind. The drugs still had her sluggish, but she was still going to give it a solid try.

"We've got this." I knew I was trying to reassure myself, but I couldn't help it.

I could feel Imp fluff her feathers in agreement.

"Three, two, one—" I slammed my body against the door.

The door caved under the force of my strength. It

crashed to the floor, and with a battle cry, I leaped on top of it as the metal slid across the floor. The soldiers lunged for me, but using the sliding door, I dodged their hands while simultaneously delivering fatal blows to the back of their necks.

Just kidding.

That's what I thought would happen. What really happened was when I slammed my shoulder into the metal door, the door fought back.

My left shoulder popped out of its socket, and I was thrown back against the opposite wall. Gritting my teeth to keep from screaming at the white-hot agony burning through my body, I used my right hand to hold my floppy left arm motionless.

Tom and Josh shouted, and the heavy thuds of their boots grew louder as they made their way toward me. Well, so much for not drawing their attention until I was out of my steel shoebox. Good thing I was good at improvising.

Waiting until I could hear their voices on the other side of the door, I pulled my legs back and slammed my sneaker-covered feet into the door with all the strength I could muster.

The door gave with a pained screech that was followed almost immediately by another screech of pain as it slammed into Josh's face. He crumpled like a puppet whose strings had been cut.

I cringed as the door crashed on top of him. He had to die, but that didn't mean I enjoyed watching it happen. It was a relief to discover the death of a chemically bonded mate wouldn't result in my death like it would with my natural mates. I shoved my emotions into a dark box in the very back of my brain, behind everything else I wanted to forget about—things like being murdered by a beetle.

Turning my attention to Tom, I saw his hand reach for the radio at his hip.

I shook my head. "I can't let you do that."

He yanked the clip from his belt, and I plowed into him. We toppled backward, landing hard on the metal floor. I swallowed my scream of pain as my shoulder popped back into place. The radio clattered across the floor and slid under Mace's motionless body.

Tom's combat boot slammed into my stomach, knocking the wind from me.

"Son of a bee sting!" I hissed.

Grabbing his gun, he brought it toward my head. I needed to end this before I was beat black and blue. I pressed my hand to his chest and called on a skill I'd first discovered in the Amazon. It crackled from my palm, surging into him with far more power than I'd anticipated.

His body lurched and twisted in the best dang worm dance move I'd ever witnessed. I was tossed away from him, slamming into Trevor's unconscious body. It was like his crotch was a magnet for my shoe, because it connected... hard enough to make him wheeze even though he shouldn't be feeling any pain. We really needed to stop meeting like this before I forced Trevor's baby-making factories into early retirement.

Rolling to my side, I gave Trevor an apologetic kiss on

the cheek. I would definitely make it up to him later. I just didn't plan to tell him what exactly I was making up for.

I shoved to my feet, wincing at the throb in my shoulder. Both soldiers lay motionless, but I still moved to take their pulses. I didn't want to be an idiot from a horror movie and have them jump-scare me later. Like I'd suspected, they were dead.

That grim task finished, I tried to figure out which part of my plan I should focus on next. This would be easier to do if I had a more solid plan rather than my usual fly-by-the-seat-of-my-pants type of plan.

I t took longer than I liked to get the cuffs off the men. Snapping the last pair, I stood, stretching my aching back. Using the back of my hand to wipe at the sweat beading my brow, I studied the nine sleeping beauties scattered around the floor.

They'd been given a massive dose of the tranq. It was going to take hours for it to wear off unless I used my magic to heal them. I could burn through the toxin in their systems, thereby reducing their recovery time. But healing all of them would take time, more time than I had. If I rushed the healing, I could end up boiling their blood by accident.

My eyes studied the wall dividing the front of the plane from the cargo area. Or did I leave my men napping and go take out the rest of the soldiers? If I waited until we landed to take out the soldiers, I would have to deal with the soldiers on the plane, as well as the ones waiting to escort us off the plane.

I was powerful, but I wasn't in perfect condition at the moment. The tranq had been burned from my system, but my body needed time to recover from the after-effects.

If I was being honest with myself, I was scared... of me. There was a new type of power humming in my veins after the bonding with Xerxes. Last time I'd been tested, I'd been ready to do whatever it took to punish the men who'd hurt those I loved. Even if it meant I hurt innocent people in the process.

If I called on my full power, could I control it? Would I be able to pull it back inside? Or would it be like trying to stuff a comforter back into the package after opening it?

I could really use the help of my mates right now, but that didn't seem to be an option. Striding to the wall, I slid my hands along it, searching for a weakness. Whoever had put the wall in place had done a fantastic job. It was seamless and sturdy.

I sagged into the nearest seat. Dropping my head into my hands, I closed my eyes. By my estimate, after escaping the metal box, taking out the two guards, and then freeing the men, I had about fifty minutes remaining before the plane touched down.

If I freed Xerxes and healed him, he could move through the wall and help me. Deciding that was my best option, I opened my eyes. Just in time to see a spider the size of a small dog scurry across my shoe.

I'm not proud of what happened next.

With the memories of my last encounter with a spider flashing through my mind in stunning 4K resolution, I screamed. That was a natural and perfectly normal response. It was less natural to burst into a human torch and run straight through the steel wall.

I wasn't thinking about anything other than escaping the hairy eight-legged nope that was also running around in a full-blown panic.

With both adrenaline and my magic surging through my body, I didn't even feel the wall when I burst through the steel like it was made of paper. The soldiers buckled in the passenger seats yelled in shock.

Not wanting to be shot, I called on my magic. It responded with a surge of power I'd not experienced before. My palms burned, and flames leaped from my hands. I caught movement from the corner of my eye. Murderous Miriam Webster had followed me into the passenger cabin. I thought it was moths that had an unhealthy addiction to flames.

"Don't come any closer!" I screamed since clearly the spider understood English and would respect my boundaries.

I was wrong. Maybe the spider spoke Spanish or French, because the not-so-itsy-bitsy-spider rushed at me, crossing boundaries like it was the spider's life purpose.

I flung out my hand, and a ball of fire slammed into the spot I'd seen the spider. Seconds later, I caught a flash of the second hairiest legs I'd ever seen... beaten only by my legs during winter. Crap. Now that I wasn't single, I'd have to shave year-round from now on.

I flung another ball of fire in the spider's direction but

missed again. This was confirmed when the spider darted across the floor in front of me. With a scream, I rampaged through the cabin, cleverly disguised as a five-foot-tall roman candle. Throwing up both hands, I blindly slung fire at everything that moved.

Screams rang in my ears, and the cabin lights flickered before cutting off completely. The plane rolled to the left, and I desperately grabbed for anything to stop myself, but my fingers slipped. My body went airborne, and I experienced a terrifying moment of weightlessness.

The plane abruptly banked to the right, and I was no longer weightless. I would have slammed into the opposite side of the plane if not for the pair of hands that plucked me from the air and pulled me into the nearest seat.

I screamed.

"Ryls! It's me, Willard!"

His voice penetrated my terror-induced fog. I looked down at the hands around my waist, surprised to feel some of my anxiety drain away. His touch was calming me, not as much as the touch of my other mates, but there was still a noticeable difference. I also came to the realization that I was naked, thanks to my fire burning away my clothes.

POP!

No, no, no, no.

Sparkling confetti drifted around us.

Willard winced, yanking his hand off me like he'd been burned. My stomach dropped to the floor, and my heartbeat thundered in my ears. I'd branded him as mine.

"What just happened?" Willard rotated his hand this way and that to look at his freshly tattooed palm.

"Now is not the time for me to explain," I squeaked, trying to swallow my panic. As far as I was concerned, there would never be a good time for this conversation. How was I supposed to tell him that while the lab-created bond we shared wasn't real, the one I'd just branded on his skin was?

Willard shoved me to the floor. Well, that didn't bode well for our future conversation.

"What the...?" I trailed off as a knife whistled through the air where I'd been sitting.

Willard had seen the knife and moved me out of the way just in time. He grabbed the man's arm, twisting it until the man released the blade, and it clattered under the seats. Fantastic. They'd just armed my eight-legged would-be assassin.

I screamed, scooting back as the knife-wielding soldier crashed to the floor next to me, his neck broken. My eyes shot to Willard, afraid he'd been hurt.

"Behind you!" he warned, lunging toward me.

I looked over my shoulder at the short, balding soldier. He'd been the creep to chain me to a chair in the villa's courtyard. My skin crawled remembering the way he'd touched my skin. Fury burned deep in my chest. Lifting his gun, he aimed for my head. Willard threw himself in front of me.

Were all men idiots? Or just the ones around me? Even I knew firing guns in an airplane would lead to serious issues. It was a wonder my fire-throwing hadn't already sent us hurtling to Earth. And if Willard was going to be my mate, he had to learn that I wasn't keen on my mates risking their lives to save me.

With a burst of speed, I shoved myself off the floor. I slammed hard into Willard's body, knocking him out of the line of fire. At the same time, I slung a burst of fire at the soldier. It consumed him, turning the man to ash at a speed I could only describe as supernatural.

My eyes darted around, taking in the dim cabin. It was lit only by the fire burning through the seats. The walls and floor were blackened, and several of the inner window-panes had cracked. Piles of ash and partially burned bodies littered the seats and floor.

I looked back at Willard. He sat up, touching the cut on his forehead where his head had met a metal armrest on one of the seats. There wasn't a single burn or reddened skin on him.

This made no sense. Confused, I stared at the remains of the men my fire had devoured. They'd claimed to be chemically bonded to me, just like Willard. If my fire didn't recognize a lab-created bond, then why was Willard unharmed? He'd grabbed me, holding me against him when I'd been on fire, but it hadn't hurt him. And that was before my magic decided to complicate things by claiming him.

The plane tilted toward the ground, forcing me to grab a nearby seat in order to steady myself. Who was flying this plane? Spinning around, I watched in horror as the pilot's body slid onto the floor. He was either a ridiculously sound sleeper, or he was dead.

A hand grabbed my ankle, yanking me to the ground. My chin banged against the floor with a force that rattled my head. Twisting in his grasp, I kicked him hard in the face with my free foot. He grunted, but didn't release my other leg.

"You aren't going to mess this up for all of us." He pulled me toward him, and I blasted him hard with my fire.

I closed my eyes, not wanting to see his skin melt as my fire burned him alive. "Willard?" My voice wobbled.

His fingers brushed against my cheek, reassuring and cool. "I'm here. What do you need?"

Turning my head so I wouldn't see the dead man, I faced Willard. "A pilot. We need a pilot."

Willard looked past me to where the pilot continued enjoying his eternal nap. His eyes widened, and his face paled.

"You can't fly a plane, can you?" I asked, already knowing the answer.

He shook his head, still staring at the pilot.

I chewed on my lip. Which of my mates could fly a plane? I didn't know, which meant I was going to have to guess and hope I picked right.

"I can," Mace slurred.

Both Willard and my head snapped toward the cargo hold. Mace was crawling through the doorway into the cabin. His body swayed, still struggling with the effects of the tranquilizer. Unfortunately, beggars couldn't be picky, and he was my best option at the moment.

"Let's get him to the front, and then I'll try to heal him," I ordered.

Willard was already heading toward Mace before I'd even finished speaking. Kicking free of the bones holding my leg, I pushed myself to my feet. I moved to follow him, but stopped at a sharp pain in my neck.

"Ow." I slapped my hand over my neck and found a syringe sticking out of it. Spinning around, I came face to face with a thing of nightmares. And no, it wasn't the spider.

Commander Hensel, a.k.a. Scar-face, stood in front of me. Except his scar was gone. It had been scorched off by my fire, along with half his face. His clothes were hanging on by a thread. My throat tightened at the sight of his burned upper chest and arm.

"You didn't think you were just going to kill my men and escape, did you?" Hensel took a step toward me.

I raised my hand, planning to blast him with fire, but nothing happened. My hand was no longer on fire. I called for my magic, but nothing happened.

"You can keep trying, but I've just given you a dose of tranquilizer that is powerful enough to take down ten elephants. You are going to be out for a while." Hensel smiled a gruesome half-smile. He must be in shock to not feel the pain of his injuries.

Hensel grabbed my arm and shoved me into a half-burned chair. His attention was drawn to Willard as he dragged Mace down the aisle.

"Willard? What are you doing?" the commander asked in confusion.

He must have been knocked out and missed Willard helping us.

Willard's gaze bounced between Hensel and me, his brain working to figure out the next step. Dropping my head back against the seat, I turned my face so Hensel couldn't see my lips. I mouthed 'shh' at him.

I needed Willard to get Mace to the front of the plane, or we were all going to die. Hensel was mine to deal with.

"With the pilot dead, I was trying to find someone to fly the plane. This shifter knows how." Willard's voice hardened as he spoke, and his eyes grew distant and cold. He'd slipped back on the mask he'd worn for so long.

Hensel nodded. "Smart thinking. Get him to the front and keep an eye on him. Don't let him change course."

I snorted. We would be lucky if he was able to land the plane at all with the amount of damage I'd caused.

Willard hesitated. Finally, he turned away from me and half-supported, half-dragged Mace toward the front of the plane. I was left alone to deal with Hensel, and I only had about thirty minutes left to do it.

*H*ensel snapped one cuff to my limp hand and the second cuff to the metal plane chair. Leaning down, he pulled a blade from his boot and held it to my neck.

"We are so close to the facility, and I won't let you cause me any more issues." Hensel's knife trailed down my neck and between my bare breasts. He paused at my stomach, just above my belly.

Leaning in, he pressed his lips hard against my mouth in a bruising kiss. I gagged at the smell of burned human flesh. At the same time, he pressed the blade into my stomach. A scream ripped up my throat, but I swallowed it and tightened my lips, refusing to give him access to my open mouth.

Hensel dragged the knife down my stomach and sent searing pain ricocheting through my body. I could feel the warm, wet feeling of blood sliding down my stomach.

Pulling back from me, he smirked. "There. That should

keep you out of trouble. This wound will keep you weak, but it won't kill you—at least not until after we land. Can't have you regenerating and causing more trouble before we have you locked up."

Satisfied I wasn't going anywhere, he moved to check the bodies of the men scattered around the plane.

"You've killed all but three of my men." He hissed through his teeth. "These guys were my best men. Such a pity. And for what? You and your men are still my captives."

Hensel walked down the aisle toward the back of the plane. I tried to respond, but my tongue felt too big for my mouth, and my lips refused to move. No matter how much I fought it, the edges of my vision grew darker.

The plane wobbled. I leaned to the side, trying to see the front of the plane. Willard had managed to get Mace to the pilot's seat. Mace swayed to the side, nearly toppling from the chair. Willard was quick to shove him back into the seat and give him a hard shake.

They needed my help, and I was sitting here useless, slowly bleeding out.

A groan came from the cargo bay. Inch by painstaking inch, I leaned to the side and looked into the cargo area. Hensel held several pairs of cuffs in his hands as he strolled around the men.

He stopped in front of Knox and delivered a vicious kick to the jaguar shifter. But he wasn't finished. His boot slammed into Knox over and over. Tears ran down my cheeks, and my body shook with silent sobs. My vocal cords refused to respond to my brain's commands. Hensel looked directly at me, letting me see the depths of his malicious cruelty.

Unable to watch and not wanting to give Hensel the pleasure of seeing how much he was affecting me, I slowly turned back in my chair. My body slumped to the side, and I was too exhausted to pull myself up.

The plane was still wobbling, but it had mostly steadied. Mace and Willard were still trying to save the mission, yet here I sat, doing nothing but slowly dying.

I was the last Phoenix, and because of that, these men who loved me had been drawn into a mess they didn't ask for. I'd failed them. I hadn't been fast enough, strong enough, or smart enough to do what needed to be done.

We would land and then be locked away from each other for who knew how long. The train would crash, and more lives would be lost. And there was nothing I could do.

The dark thing moved under my skin as though reminding me there was another option. Urging me to call it out to play. Each time I bonded with a mate, I grew stronger. More powerful. But this thing that lurked inside me after bonding with Xerxes was on a different level. I doubted I could control it if I were in perfect condition, so how in the heck was I supposed to do it was drugged and dying?

"Ten minutes until we land!" Willard called out, voice urgent.

It looked like I didn't have a choice.

This time I didn't call for my magic, I ordered it to do my bidding.

I WAS MORE than a little afraid the magic would explode out of me and blow up the plane. Instead, it uncoiled itself, languid and unhurried. As the power pumped through me, my anxiousness faded away to be replaced by calm assurance.

The burn in my stomach intensified, and I cracked open my eyes to see a soft glow coming from my stomach, and the edges of the wound stitching themselves back together.

I barely managed to bite back a scream as my blood began to boil. The magic was burning through the tranquilizer in my system at a breathtaking rate. I was thankful to feel my head clearing and the effects of the drug disappearing, but holy guacamole did it hurt.

I was breathing hard by the time the wound healed, and the drug was cleansed from my system. Unfortunately, I didn't have time to catch my breath. I'd probably lost three minutes, which meant I had about seven left until we landed. Plenty of time.

I stood, the cuffs around my wrists disintegrating into dust. Jaw clenched and power rippling under my skin, I made my way to the cargo hold. Hensel leaned over Dagger's body, working the cuffs around my jaguar's wrists.

"Hensel," I snarled.

Hensel slowly stood to his full height, confusion and wariness flitting across his features. He took in my healed stomach, and then I saw the fear. "That's impossible!"

I stepped closer. "I've heard that before."

Hensel pulled a gun from his belt and aimed it at Dagger's head. "Step any closer, and I'll put a bullet through his head."

"I'm never going to let you hurt another person. Especially not my mates." I moved across the room so fast he didn't even see it coming and knocked the gun from his hand.

"Willard!" Hensel's eyes widened in terror, and he called out for the only other soldier on the plane who was conscious.

"He's not coming. Willard is mine."

Hensel's attention was drawn to the impromptu door I'd blasted into the wall. Willard stepped through it and came to stand behind me. His hand curled around my neck, and the commander grinned in triumph, believing he'd won.

Willard's hand gripped my jaw. He gently turned my face to the side and brushed a soft kiss against my lips. "I'm yours."

Hensel cursed and lunged at me. I pressed my hands to his chest and released a surge of power that sizzled through his body with more force than a lightning strike. It reduced him to a pile of ash in the blink of an eye.

With him out of the way, I turned to the men. Xerxes,

Anzac, Jett, Dagger, Trevor, Knox, Lee, and Jackson were slowly waking up, but they still had too much of the drug in their systems. Not having the time to heal them individually, I had Willard help me push them together.

There was a groan from the passenger cabin, and Willard's head snapped in that direction. "I better take care of a few things."

Watching Willard head toward the semi-conscious soldiers, relief welled up inside me. I was more than happy to accept his help.

Trusting Willard to handle the last of the enemy soldiers, I kneeled on the floor by my guys—my family. I pressed a hand on Jett's chest and the other hand on Dagger's back. Taking a deep breath, I sent a wave of my power into the men. It surged from one man to another like an electrical charge.

My body burst into flames, and sweat trickled down my spine as I worked to send just the right amount of magic to heal them, but not fry them. I yanked my hands away as soon as the drug had been burned from their systems and their bodies had been healed.

Dagger was the first to open his eyes, and he gave me an appreciative smile. "What a gorgeous sight to wake up to."

Laughing in relief, I brushed my lips across his cheek. "You guys should buckle into those seats. We are about to land. I'll be back." I hurried to the front of the plane. Mace needed me.

"Where's Hensel?" Mace brushed a strand of hair from my face.

"He's dead. The rest of the guys are waking up. You should buckle in before we land." I rested my hands on his chest and sent magic pouring into him.

Mace's arm wrapped around my waist and hauled me down onto his thigh. "I love you."

I wrapped my arms around his neck, fitting my body against his chest. My power was still surging through him, devouring the last traces of the tranquilizer.

"We need to buckle in." His voice was raspy against my ear, and I shivered with delight. "Straddle me."

I didn't argue and did as he instructed.

Mace pulled the straps around us. "It may get a little rough."

Those were words I never wanted to hear while flying, so why did my body respond with excitement?

The pull in my chest that was constantly pushing me to bond with all my mates had turned from a constant tickle to a demanding ache. I pressed my lips to his neck and teased the tip of my tongue to his skin, loving the taste of him.

Mace purred encouragement, further exciting the wildness taking root inside me. My magic had finished its task, and I tried to call it back, but I couldn't. The intimacy of my power surging between our bodies was addictive.

My thighs tightened around Mace as much as possible, which was a challenge considering he was essentially a modern-day giant. I trailed kisses on every bit of exposed skin.

"I don't want to stop." I rocked my hips against him.

Mace's chest rumbled. "Then don't stop."

So I didn't, and Mace had to figure out how to land the plane with a sex-crazed Phoenix strapped across his lap. He was pretty good at multitasking, it turned out. Within minutes, we were bouncing down the short runway. I'd never been a fan of bumpy landings, but this one had me reconsidering my stance. I had to bury my face in Mace's neck to keep from groaning at how incredible it felt. The instant Mace switched off the engines, his lips found mine, and he kissed me with his own raw need.

"Guys?" Dagger's voice pulled me back to the present. He touched my shoulder to get my attention. "Guys! Soldiers are gathering outside the cargo door, waiting for it to lower. I know it's hard—" Dagger snickered at his pun while wiggling his eyebrows at us. At a sharp look from me, he sighed and continued. "But we need to deal with this before they get impatient."

I knew Dagger was right, but it was impossible to think clearly with the hammering in my head demanding I claim Mace.

"They are trying to lower it manually from the outside!" Knox yelled from the cargo hold.

The straps pressing into my back fell away. "Come on, Ryls. We need to get everyone armed and into position."

Mace broke the kiss, pulling away. Reluctantly, I called my magic back from him. It swirled inside me, restless and irritated. The thing just beneath my skin unfurled in agitation. All that combined with my own anger over being denied my mate again made for an explosive mix of emotions. I'd taken everything life threw at me without complaining... mostly.

It was my turn to be a little selfish. The only things standing in the way of bonding with Mace were the soldiers outside and the ones guarding the facility. I stood from Mace's lap.

"There's no need to arm anyone. This won't take long." I released the hold I kept on my magic, and delighted in the wild power cascading inside me as I dropped through the floor.

15

WILLARD

"*I*'ve never felt so confused, turned on, and terrified at the same time." I stared at the hole Ryls had just dropped through.

"Join the club." Mace punched my shoulder.

The man didn't know his own strength, and I stumbled back. I think he intended it to be playful, but I wasn't entirely sure. When I'd helped Mace to the front of the plane, I'd given him a quick rundown of what was going on, letting him know I was working to help Ryls escape these men.

"Will I get used to it?" I asked, hurrying after him toward the cargo bay.

Mace's chest rumbled with a dark chuckle. "Unlikely. Amaryllis likes to color outside the lines. If you ask her to think inside the box, she'll ask, 'What box?' She's a wild card, and we just try to keep up."

"That's not reassuring," I mumbled, twisting my hand to look at the mark on my hand.

"Where's Ryls?" Anzac asked as we stepped through the hole and into the cargo hold.

"And why is this piece of pond scum still breathing?" Dagger took a menacing step toward me.

Mace reached back and grabbed my wrist, yanking me in front of him. He held up my hand, showing the mark Ryls had left on my skin. The silence that followed was deafening.

Yanking my hand away, I rubbed my wrist. The men still didn't move, and I eyed them warily, not trusting that they wouldn't attack me. I wouldn't even blame them if they did try to kill me. If I were in their shoes, it's exactly what I'd do.

Jett cleared his throat. "Did she ask before she marked you? Or was it an accident?"

My brow creased. "She seemed surprised when it happened."

Knox smiled and shook his head. "She's going to feel so guilty."

I didn't understand. "Why would she feel guilty?"

"Because she didn't ask you first." Mace didn't look up from where he was punching buttons into a panel to lower the cargo bay door. "She still doesn't realize how precious a gift it is to be claimed as her mate."

"And because she doesn't understand that we'd already chosen her before she marked us." Xerxes handed me a gun, and I pulled the strap over my head.

I agreed with them, although I still felt like I was missing something big.

"Where is Ryls?" Anzac repeated.

A volley of gunfire exploded outside the plane. Crouching down, we spun around toward the cargo door, guns raised.

"Out there," Mace answered.

As the door lowered, I spotted Amaryllis. It would have been hard to miss her. She looked like a fairy tucked safely inside rose petals... if the rose petals were on fire.

The soldiers were unloading clip after clip of bullets, but the bullets fell harmlessly to the ground, not penetrating her fiery shield. Her face wasn't one of fear—she looked bored. When she spotted us, her expression changed to one of a frustrated parent with a naughty toddler.

A group of soldiers spotted us and turned their guns in our direction. Ryls caught the shift in their position, and she threw a wall of fire up between the soldiers and us.

Anzac cursed. "She's blocked us in."

I spun in a slow circle. Sure enough, a wall of fire surrounded us on all sides. Ryls had put us in time-out.

With us out of the way, Ryls ran toward the soldiers. Reaching the first cluster of men, she leaped into the middle of them. Fiery wings ripped from her back, and she spun in a tight circle, her wings setting everything they touched on fire. My ears rang with the sounds of gunfire and the screams of dying men.

Something shot into the air like a firecracker.

I craned my neck back to watch its trajectory. "What is that?"

"Imp." Anzac's voice was tight.

"Oh, man. Things are about to get a lot crazier." Knox sounded gleeful.

I didn't know what an imp was, but I was about to get a crash course. Literally.

The ball of fire fell toward the plane, falling through the roof and disappearing inside.

"Get down!" Xerxes shouted.

I was shoved to the ground just as the plane detonated like a bomb. Burning shrapnel was sent slicing through the air like flaming missiles. We were protected thanks to the cage Ryls had stuck us in. The same could not be said for everyone else on the field.

Around us, the world looked like an apocalypse. Dark smoke billowed from what was left of the plane. The grass, which had been tall and green this morning, had been burned to the ground, leaving behind only blackened earth. Ryls was a blur of glittering gold and red as she moved through the men. She left nothing but embers and ash in her wake.

The ball of fire that had destroyed the plane swirled around her, destroying anything she missed. It was incredible. She was incredible.

"Looks like Will just fell even harder for our girl." Jett grinned at me.

I kept my features emotionless, not ready for them to see just how accurate his assessment was. I'd fallen in love with her when I was assigned to guard her. That entire mission had been torture.

When it was all over, Ryls let the fiery wall around us

disappear into the ground. The thing called 'Imp' darted toward the facility. I winced at the damage it was going to do.

Lee and Jackson must have had a similar thought because they leaped to their feet and ran after her. "Stop, Imp! We need those records!"

Ryls sighed and pinched the bridge of her nose. Her skin glowed with light and static crackled across her skin. Spinning on her heel, she stomped after Jackson and Lee.

"Come on. We need to clear the building of threats." Grabbing our gear, we rushed after her retreating back.

"Stupid universe is always clam-jamming me," Ryls grumbled.

The guys burst into laughter behind me.

I wasn't sure I'd heard her correctly. "Did you say *clam-jamming?*"

Ryls threw up her hands, then jumped when fire leaped from her hands and set a tree on fire. "Clam-jammed, beaver-dammed, muffin-muzzled, bushwhacked, box-locked..."

Her words were drowned out by our howls of laughter.

"Please, stop!" Knox begged. Tears ran down his face, and he clutched his sides.

"I'm done with this." Ryls burst into flames and raced toward the building.

ENTERING THE FACILITY, I expected to find everything on fire, parts of the ceiling collapsed, and walls missing. Instead, everything was pristine and eerily quiet.

"Ryls!" Trevor shouted.

There was no response. Fear chilled my blood.

"We are going to clear this place room by room until we find her," Anzac barked.

Nodding, we fell in line and followed him in a crouch down the hall. I joined the military immediately after turning eighteen, so taking orders and carrying out tactical missions was second nature. We cleared room after room. It wasn't until we opened the eighth door that we found Lee. He was busily typing away on a laptop.

"Lee, where is everyone? Where is Ryls?" Anzac demanded.

"Your mate tore through here like a hurricane. Most of the guards were outside to meet the plane. There were only a couple guarding the exits and a handful of lab staff. She and Jackson rounded them up and took them to the holding cells until she could decide what she wanted to do with them," Lee answered without looking up.

"Is it just me, or is she showing signs of becoming stronger?" Trevor wondered out loud.

"Oh, she is definitely getting stronger. She bonded with the Drakon, correct?" Lee's fingers flew across the keyboard as he spoke.

Xerxes nodded. "Yes, we are fully bonded."

"Every time she bonds, she unlocks more of her magic." Lee pushed away from the laptop and met our faces. "But she still hasn't bonded with Mace. So she is an incredibly powerful Phoenix who is teetering on the edge of losing control."

Mace was in front of Lee in two strides. He grabbed the smaller man's shirt and shook him frantically. "It's not too late to bond with her, right? Tell me I can still fix this!"

A slow smile spread across Lee's face. I didn't know him well, but it creeped me the frick out. Judging by the way Mace gently set him back down on the seat and the other guys took a step back, I wasn't the only one weirded out.

"We don't know enough about phoenixes for me to be one hundred percent sure, but I don't believe it's too late." The weird smile stayed fixed on Lee's face. He was enjoying this.

"Then why are you smiling like that?" Dagger asked with suspicion.

"Because Ryls's body is pushing her to complete the bonding, and her magic is likely to be unpredictable." He focused on Mace again. "You will have to grab the bull by the horns. Or, more accurately, grab the Phoenix by the tail."

Mace paled.

"I would suggest you stop wasting time." Lee shook his head and turned back to the laptop.

"Let's go find Ryls." Xerxes headed for the door, and we followed.

"Good luck," Lee called, his laughter echoing down the hall after us.

It didn't take us long to find Ryls. She was looking out a

window in the facility's break room. Her wings were wrapped around her trembling body.

"Ryls!" Mace's relief at finding her was palpable.

She turned to face us, and I forgot to breathe. Ryls was a beautiful woman even when covered in dirt, but now she looked ethereal. Crimson hair floated around her face, blowing in a non-existent wind. Light radiated from her bare skin like the warm glow from a fireplace. Her golden eyes glowed, and something predatory flickered in their depths. Electricity popped and crackled, dancing across her skin and reminding me of lightning during a summer storm.

While I hoped one day I'd get a chance to make love to Amaryllis, I was glad I wasn't the one who needed to calm her down today.

"You're up." Dagger clapped Mace on the back and whispered, "Go get 'em, tiger—er, jaguar."

Mace swallowed hard, straightened his shoulders, and stepped toward her.

Ryls's fiery wings wrapped tighter around her. "Stop, I don't want to hurt you." Her voice cracked, and my heart broke. She was scared.

"You won't hurt me, love." Mace took another step toward her.

"What if we bond, and I can't control it?" Ryls pleaded.

Mace swept her into his arms. "Then I will help you. And if I need backup, we can always tag them in." He jerked his chin in our direction.

Ryls winced, her face crumpling in pain.

"What's wrong?" Mace searched her body for an injury.

"I've wanted you for so long. That need is getting more demanding." She looked away from him. "And more painful."

Mace growled. "Use me, love. Take what you need from me. Let me help you."

Ryls grabbed his face between her hands and kissed him like her life depended on it. Mace stumbled back onto the couch. Ryls shifted in his arms and straddled his lap.

She had her wings folded tight against her back, and when Mace's hands settled on her hips, I was reminded of how big he was, and just how petite Ryls was. When Mace's hands slid down to cup the perfect curves of her butt, my pants suddenly felt a size smaller.

It was sensual watching them together, but it also felt wrong, like I was viewing something that was supposed to. "Should we leave them? Give them privacy?"

Ryls spun around on Mace's lap to face us. "No. You are all staying here. I need to know you are safe, so I don't have to worry."

Mace trailed kisses up her spine, and she arched her back with an adorable groan. "Plus, you better make sure we're not interrupted this time."

When Mace's hands slid along her ribs and cupped her breasts, the temperature in the room spiked, and my mouth went dry. This was going to be the best kind of torture.

16

RYL8

I was doing my best to hide how much pain I was in. It was like an insidious vine twisting through my body and coiling around my organs. The agony had been steadily escalating since we'd landed. Mace's hands on my bare skin were a welcome relief.

My eyes closed, and I tried to memorize every detail of how it felt to have his lips kissing up my spine, and his hands teasing my breasts. It was comical how the size of his hands covered so much of my skin at once, but I wasn't complaining.

I was so caught up in the feel of Mace's touch on my body I didn't hear Jett cross the room or kneel in front of me. I didn't even notice when Mace used his thick, muscular thighs to spread my legs. But I sure felt it when Jett's mouth kissed between my legs, and his tongue teased along my slit.

I yelped in shock and would have fallen from Mace's lap if he hadn't gripped my hips and held me still.

"You're not going anywhere, minx. We are going to worship your hot little body until you aren't able to walk," Mace rasped against my neck.

I quivered and felt myself grow wetter.

"Mm. She likes that idea." Jett licked me, long and slow.

As much as I didn't want reality to come crashing down on me, it did. We didn't have time to be doing this right now. "The train. I need to—"

Knox moved in front of me. "You need to stop worrying about the rest of the world. Right now, you need to take care of yourself." He bent down and kissed me.

"Besides, Jackson and Lee are working out the details of the train. Let them do their work," Xerxes reassured me from where he leaned against the wall. His eyes glowed with hunger.

I glanced toward Willard, my accidental mate. He'd slid to the floor, and sweat trickled down his face as he watched my mates pleasure me. Jett's tongue thrust inside my tight walls, and a low moan escaped me. Willard's pupils dilated with lust.

"Naughty girl. You like it when your mates watch you be pleasured, don't you?" Xerxes's voice pitched low. He was just as turned on as I was.

I tried to respond, but I couldn't do more than whimper.

Mace's teeth nipped my shoulder. "Use your words."

"Y-y-yes," I moaned.

Mace's teeth pressed harder into my skin, sending chills rippling across my skin. Jett groaned, his tongue thrusting harder inside me. Mace's fingers dug into my hips as he rocked my hips on Jett's face.

Knox dropped to his knees beside Jett. He wasted no time sucking my breast into his scorching hot mouth. Not wanting to be left out, Dagger dropped to the floor on the opposite side of Jett. I gasped when his mouth lavished attention on my neglected breast.

Through hazy eyes, I took in Willard sitting on the floor, looking like he was running a fever. He was discretely trying to rub his hand across the tent in his pants. When he caught me watching, he blushed. For better or worse, this man was part of my circle. He had a lot to adjust to.

"Willard. Remove your clothes," Xerxes ordered, causing my eyes to snap to his gaze. There was a wickedness lurking in his eyes, and the magic straining to escape my skin was inexplicably drawn to it.

Willard spluttered. "Excuse me?"

Xerxes didn't look away from me as he answered. "Ryls desires it. She wants to see what this is doing to your body."

My dragon was right. I wanted to see the evidence of my mates' lust.

Willard hesitated for a minute, then pulled his shirt over his head and slowly kicked off his pants. The human wasn't wearing underwear, and his hard length sprung free.

Jett purred. "Don't stop there, X. She likes that."

My eyes slid to Anzac.

"You too, Anzac," Xerxes ordered.

Anzac didn't share any of Willard's shyness and dropped his cargo pants with a relieved sigh.

"Now stroke yourselves. Nice and slow." Xerxes's voice reverberated around the room, but his eyes never left mine.

Both Willard and Anzac gripped their stiff erections. Squeezing and sliding, they ran their hands up and down their lengths. Veins bulged on their hands and arms, and their breathing grew erratic. The demanding hunger inside me intensified.

I fumbled with the front of Dagger and Knox's pants. They must have been eager for my touch, because right as I decided to set them on fire like I'd done to Xerxes's shirt, both men dropped their pants for me.

I wrapped one hand around each erection. They jerked at my touch and moaned against my skin. The sharp prick of Mace's fangs on the back of my neck told me the jaguar shifter's beast was pushing forward, urging him to mate me.

Mace was still clothed, but I could feel the hard rod in his pants pressing against my backside. His hands continued to grind me into Jett's hungry mouth and, shifting his hips, Mace slid his length in the valley between my butt cheeks.

"Jett, you better get on with it, or I am going to lose it," Mace snarled.

My eyes rolled back in my head when his tongue shifted and grew longer. The increased friction from the rough surface of his tongue was enough to send my body rushing toward my climax.

You're delicious, my little bird. I want more. Jett's silky voice caressed my mind as intimately as his tongue flicked across my slick heat.

"Jett." I gasped his name, my body tightening with the need for release.

Give it to me, Jett demanded.

This time when Jett purred, he sent the reverberations through his tongue as well. He'd just turned his tongue into a freaking vibrator, and I didn't stand a chance. I came apart on Jett's tongue with a scream.

The pleasure was intense to the point of near pain, and I tried to escape from Jett's probing tongue, but Mace and Jett weren't having it.

Mace held my hips still and even spread me wider to give Jett better access. "Don't deny Jett. He earned his prize."

Jett growled, grabbing my thighs and burying his tongue deeper. He was a demanding cat trying to lick up every drop of cream. It was too much, and my second orgasm broke without warning.

Knox and Dagger roared their own release, their erections jerking in my hands.

I looked down, bewildered at their sudden release.

"That's interesting," Xerxes murmured. "It's your hands, Ryls. You are vibrating with power, and the electrical lightning sparking across your hands stimulates them to an instant orgasm."

Dagger and Knox collapsed to the floor, their bodies still twitching.

"They're okay, right?" I asked, biting my lip.

Mace's chest rumbled with laughter. "They are more than okay."

"Best orgasm of my life," Knox wheezed.

"Same, bro," Dagger choked out.

Looking down at my hands, I turned them, watching my veins glow beneath my skin. I wasn't sure what was happening, but I knew things were changing inside me at a frightening pace. Instinctually, I recognized this was only the start of the shifting magic inside me.

A big piece of the puzzle clicked into place. Reality hit me like a frying pan to the face. My body was a battery that's never been fully charged. I'd been starving myself by depriving myself of my mates. For the past months, I'd only been taking the bare minimum, and it was enough to keep me alive, but not enough to complete the changes.

Angry growls came from around the room.

Mace's hand clamped around my throat, and his tongue traced the sensitive curve of my ear. "You aren't leaving this room until you have taken all that you need."

"I don't know what will happen." I turned fearful, pleading eyes to Trevor, hoping my gentle mate would understand.

Trevor pushed away from the wall and sauntered toward me. Putting his hand on Jett's shoulder, Trevor pushed Jett back on his heels. This made room for Trevor to stand in front of me.

Bending, Trevor delved two fingers inside me, and I moaned at his touch. Locking eyes with me, he slid his fingers out and raised them to his mouth. I watched in stunned silence as he licked them clean. My pulse pounded in my ears, and my body pulsed with need.

"Mmm, perfection. I think Mace needs a taste. Give him one." Trevor's tongue slid along his lip, and I wished his tongue was on my body.

"What? How?" It was hard to talk with my vocal cords tight and raw.

Trevor locked his fingers around my wrist and guided my hand to the apex of my thighs. "Touch yourself."

Challenge glinted in Trevor's eyes, and I realized his beast had pushed forward. He wanted to play? Game on.

I leaned back against Mace's chest and rolled my hips so Trevor could watch my finger trace my entrance before slipping inside. Jett groaned.

Trevor hadn't thought I'd do it, and now his jaw hung slack, and his chest heaved. I raised a brow and smirked. Checkmate, baby.

Shaking his head to clear it of the fog, Trevor took a step back and settled into a large armchair. Eyes aglow, he returned my smirk. "Feed him."

My cheeks burned, and I barely hid the shock from my face. What was wrong with my mates? Had they all lost their ever-loving minds? Trevor wasn't even fully comfortable being in the room when I was with my other mates.

His gryphon bonded with you on the beach. For lack of a better word, he's pushing to play with you in this form, Xerxes answered my unspoken question.

Just because Trevor's beast wanted it didn't mean Trevor did, though. It wouldn't be fair to take advantage of this tempting moment to push Trevor's boundaries. Not while Trevor was fighting for control.

Xerxes's dark chuckle drifted across the room. *Trevor isn't fighting his beast. It's the opposite, beautiful. He's allowing his shifter side more control. Trevor wants this, but doesn't know how to do it on his own.*

That was all I needed to hear. I slid my fingers from me and held them up. Trevor's pupils shifted to slits, and he inhaled deeply. Turning my head, I met Mace's jaguar eyes.

Before I could ask, Mace had sucked my fingers into his mouth. His tongue swirled around each finger, savoring my taste. Mace finally released his hold on my fingers, but at the last minute, he caught the tip of my finger between his teeth. His canines were descended, and I thought he might be preparing to eat my finger, but he released it.

"I could taste you all day, but I need to be inside you." Mace thrust against my backside, letting me feel the truth of his words.

My eyes were drawn to Jett, who'd decided to relax on the floor, propped up on his elbows while his eyes took in everything. His shirt was gone, but he still wore his dark cargo pants. My mouth watered at the outline of his erection straining against the pants.

Wanting to drive my mates crazy, I slipped off the couch onto the floor and crawled up Jett's body, and settled between his legs. Unable to help myself, I brushed my fingers across the fabric and let my fire devour the fabric. Task finished, I called my magic back to me and grinned at the man who was bare in front of me.

Dropping my head, I took Jett's length in my mouth, slow and deep. Jett hissed. "Ryls. You feel so good."

Releasing him with a wet pop, I looked over my shoulder at Mace. Raising my butt, I wiggled it. "What are you waiting for?"

Mace ripped his clothes off and settled between my legs so fast I was fairly confident he broke the sound barrier.

With a man his size stretching my legs apart, I was giving him quite an eyeful. I flushed, but my body's demands were too loud for me to back out now.

I took Jett in my mouth again, teasing the head of his erection. That was until Mace slammed into me with a single hard thrust, and I was shoved forward, and Jett's length was buried deep in my throat.

Mace groaned. "I have dreamed of this moment, but it is so much better than I imagined."

I hummed. It was hard to talk with your mouth full.

Mace slid from me and leaned forward. "You okay, Ryls?"

I let Jett pop from my mouth. With Mace no longer inside me, pain twisted my gut, and my eyes watered. My body was determined to make sure Mace and I completed the bond this time.

"Ryls? What's wrong?" Jett grabbed my chin, tight lines of worry around his eyes.

"Pain. Need Mace," I whispered, trying and failing to breathe through the pain.

Jett caught on quickly. "Mace, get your prick back in her and bang her brains out."

Mace stilled behind me, not sure what was going on.

"NOW!" Jett bellowed.

That prodded Mace into action, and he buried himself inside me, stretching me to the point I feared I'd be ruined after this. The pain eased enough for me to suck in a deep breath of air.

"That's it. Breathe, little bird," Jett coaxed, his silky voice calming my panic.

Mace pulled back, but stopped before he slid out completely. He didn't even pause before thrusting back inside. Over and over. He found the perfect rhythm; slow and rough. The agony in my stomach ebbed a little with each hard stroke.

Once the pain gave way to pleasure, I turned my attention back to Jett's body. Taking him in my mouth, I swirled my tongue around him. Jett moaned. Propping himself on one elbow, he buried the fingers of his free hand through my hair. Each time Mace rammed himself into my silken heat, I'd use the force to take Jett deep.

Jett's fingers raked across my scalp in a sensual massage, and he whispered praise. Mace's hands wrapped around my waist, his fingers almost interlacing due to our size difference. It was too much and not enough.

Mace must have sensed my need because he moved faster with each thrust. Faster and faster. Our breathing was erratic, and my body was shiny from sweat. My skin rippled as the thing inside me tested its boundaries.

Lightning no longer danced across my skin. Instead, it was collecting inside me, causing every cell in my body to vibrate with a magical charge. It was steadily growing stronger. Fear shot through my brain. Was I going to detonate?

Guys, we may have a problem— I sent through the mental link.

At the same time, Mace groaned. "Ryls, I don't know what's happening, but it feels incredible."

Jett's fingers tangled tighter in my hair, and he thrust into my mouth, no longer able to hold still. Lust and desperation twisted his handsome features. "Don't stop. Oh. Please, don't stop."

Mace was frantically pounding into me. With a distinctly feline growl, he lifted my knees off the floor and tilted my hips to bury himself deeper. The new angle caused him to hit a sensitive spot I didn't know I had. My eyes crossed so far I thought they'd be stuck forever, and magic surged inside me.

"Again. Mace. Again," I begged, only to have Jett pull my mouth back down on his hard erection.

Eager to please, Mace gripped my hips and effortlessly held me suspended as he drilled into me. I wrapped my legs as best I could around his hips. With my mouth wrapped around Jett's length, and my derriere off the ground, it was the weirdest—but most amazing—game of wheelbarrow I'd ever taken part in.

I made it twenty seconds before I was screaming as orgasmic bliss stole away my hearing and sight. All I could see, feel, or hear for several heartbeats was intense pleasure.

Jett stiffened and growled my name as he came. I yelped as I was yanked away from his pulsing erection. Mace was snarling and growling. He stood, lifting me so he could sheath himself inside me again. Without warning, his fangs sank into the back of my neck. He tried to thrust inside me again, but his erection was shifting, and he barely fit. I yelped, and he rumbled a growl.

As his length sank deeper, it grew thicker. I moaned as the rounded barbs massaged my walls. How could this feel so good?

"We need to do something. Mace has lost control. He has to finish the mating, or we have to knock him out," Anzac hissed at Xerxes.

"No!" I gasped. "Don't knock him out. He needs this. We need this."

"I can't stand by while he hurts you! You weren't meant to take our size or barbs. It's a miracle the rest of us didn't hurt you when we lost control. But Mace is so much bigger than you, and with his control gone, he could badly injure you without realizing it." Anzac took a step toward me, but Xerxes shoved past him.

Xerxes approached the growling jaguar shifter with confidence. "Mace, let me help."

Mace yanked my back hard against his chest. "Mine." The single word was spoken around his fangs, still buried in my neck.

Xerxes's veins began to glow. "You can mate her, but I'll not allow you to hurt her. I'm going to help, or we are going to have a problem."

"Fine," Mace snarled against my neck. "Hurry."

Xerxes stepped forward and caught my face between his hands. "I need you to breathe, love. Relax."

Easy for him to say. Xerxes wasn't the one being impaled on a prickly penis.

Xerxes's hand moved to my clit, and I moaned. "Relax, love. You are too tense. Focus on my breathing."

I tried to match my breathing to Xerxes's and the sensations his touch was sending through me.

"Good girl," Xerxes praised.

Mace pulled back and then slid in an inch. Instead of pain, I felt pleasure.

"That's it." Xerxes's finger was providing just the right amount of friction, and I felt my orgasm building. These men were determined to kill me.

Mace slid out and then pushed in with a single stroke, not stopping until I'd taken all of him. The barbs held his erection in place, and I felt him swell.

"Mine!" Mace roared his relief as he claimed my body and soul.

I knew the instant our bond was complete.

Because that was when I electrocuted the crap out of him.

Once we had the still unconscious Mace settled onto the floor, with a couch cushion tucked under his head, I sagged onto the couch.

"Guys, we need a game plan." I dropped my head into my hands, fighting off a wave of dizziness. I'd never had this much energy or magic flooding my system, and it was taking a lot to adjust to the way it felt.

Whatever had been inside me wanting out was motionless. It wasn't gone, though. I had the impression it was more like the thing knew it was free and no longer needed to test its boundaries. It was sated and waiting.

"I'm sure it's just your power and your body adjusting to it." Xerxes had been in my head again. He sat beside me on the couch and clasped my hand. "I've felt something similar since we bonded. There have been multiple changes for your body in the past few days, and a lot of stress. Give yourself a break."

"You're right, but that doesn't stop me from wanting answers. Or maybe I'm looking for reassurance that I'm not a danger," I confessed.

"If anything, you should be more stable now." Anzac motioned his hand around the room. "You've bonded with your fated mates. Lee said that should stabilize you."

There was an awkward pause as we all looked to Willard.

Dagger cleared his throat. "How does the chemical bond thing work?"

Willard sighed. "I wish I knew. The scientists hadn't intended to create a chemical bond between a human and a paranormal. It was a side effect, and since the formula had just been figured out right before Ryls blew the lab off the face of the earth, they hadn't had a chance to tinker with it."

Willard stood up and paced. "There's just not enough information yet."

"Do you know if there are side effects if you wait to bond?" Xerxes tucked his arm around me and leaned back against the couch.

"I don't think so." Willard hesitated, then added, "But I don't know for sure."

"What do you mean?" Trevor asked.

"I noticed small things. Most of us who felt the pull to the phoenix became slightly more irritable as the days passed. A few of the guys seemed to get sick more often. I started having migraines and trouble sleeping. But these symptoms could all be side effects of the formula and not be due to the chemical bond." Willard dropped down onto one of the armchairs. "We don't even know if the bonds would wear off, or if they are permanent."

"Why did you do it? Why would you work for them?" The words tumbled out of my mouth before I could stop them. Tears burned in my eyes, but I refused to cry.

Lifting my gaze, I met his and saw the regret and pain he carried with him. I burst into tears.

Willard rushed to my side. Kneeling in front of me, he reached out and brushed away the tears trailing down my face. "I'm so sorry, Ryls. At first, you were just my assignment. I was sent undercover to observe and collect info, both on you and what Ridgeforce was doing in their lab."

"Who are you working for?" Xerxes rubbed gentle circles on my back.

Willard sat down cross-legged at my feet. "I was recruited by a Marine General. He was approached by several senators and congressmen who'd heard rumors about a phoenix. They worried corruption and greediness would bias the way the situation got handled. The General sent five of us undercover to collect cold hard data."

Trevor opened a small refrigerator and pulled out several bottles of water. "What did they plan to do with the information?" Trevor handed the bottles out to each of us before taking a long drink of his water.

Willard picked at the label on his water bottle. "They wanted to know if the phoenix was a modern-day monster, or was harmless and being targeted by companies looking to use her for profits or study. The hope was they could make an unbiased decision and either take out the phoenix, or be her protection. At the same time, they were hoping to find out which companies were above board. Any proof we gathered could help to bring down those organizations."

"Why didn't you help her escape?" Anzac's hands were in fists.

Willard looked down, resting his chin on his chest. "You guys know how missions work. We'd spent years working on this one and getting me into a position where I was trusted and had access to private documents."

"Yeah. We've been in that position before." Knox spoke from where he still reclined on the floor. He was uncharacteristically serious, and I knew he was remembering what went down in the jungle when their mission had been their top priority.

Willard lifted his eyes. "Ryls, when I was assigned to guard you, it was just a mission. Observe and report back. Simple. But it got a lot more complicated when I started falling for you. Your endless optimism, your quick wit, your beautiful smile..."

I couldn't believe what I was hearing.

"I fell in love with you." Willard's neck flushed.

"Before the accident with the lab's formula and my blood?" I reiterated, struggling to understand what he was saying.

Willard answered by grabbing my hands and pulling me off the couch. I toppled into his lap.

"Will—" I yelped, but it was cut off by Willard's mouth capturing mine. He kissed me like a starving man.

I was panting when he released my lips. "Yes, Firebug. You stole my heart. I didn't need a chemical to fall in love with you, it just enhanced what I was already feeling."

I choked on a watery laugh. "It was my singing, wasn't it?"

Willard groaned. "You did that on purpose to annoy me."

"You bet I did. Pestering you, and listening to your music during those long boring hours, were the only things that kept me from losing my mind. You were grumpy, but you were my friend," I admitted, leaning forward to place a soft kiss on his lips.

"So what were you doing with the vials? Why were you trying to save the lab's research?" Anzac demanded.

Anger tightened Willard's features. "I wasn't trying to save it. My goal was to destroy it. I wanted to make sure no one else in the lab tried to sneak any of the vials out during the chaos. There were too many people around for me to destroy them without raising suspicion, so I tried to find an empty room to drop them in. Instead, the building started coming down around us, and I woke up to discover I was part of Ridgeforce's science project."

Willard searched my eyes. "I hate that I didn't protect you. If you don't want me, I will leave. I don't want you to feel guilted into accepting me because of a bond created by a lab."

I traced the tattoo I'd branded on Willard's hand.

175

"Willard, I need to tell you something." Taking a deep breath, I rushed ahead. "This marks you as mine. There isn't a way to undo it. I'm so sorry. Now, you're stuck with me, and you didn't get a choice."

Willard's arms wrapped around me, holding me tight. "You're wrong. I did get a choice, and I chose you. I'm just glad you chose me, too, Firebug."

My heart had never been so full of joy.

There was a soft knock on the door, and all our heads snapped in that direction.

"It's Lee. Is everyone decent?" Lee called.

Anzac stood and grabbed several lab coats hanging on hooks on the wall. He tossed one at me, one to Jett since I'd burned his pants, and he spread one over our Scottish sleeping beauty.

I slipped my arms into the thin gray coat and wrapped it tight around me. "Come in, Lee. We are about as covered as we can manage at the moment."

Lee pushed open the door with a bright smile. His grin grew bigger when he spotted Mace on the floor. "I warned the stubborn arse."

He took in our disheveled clothes and rolled his eyes. "I guess it's good I grabbed a couple backpacks with supplies as we left the plane when the rest of you grabbed guns. Especially since someone decided to blow it up." Lee's eyebrow raised accusingly, and he looked right at me when he said 'someone.'

"Don't look at me. That was all Imp's fault!" I protested.

Lee snorted and tossed the packs on the floor in the

middle of our little group. "Go ahead and see if you can find anything that works for you. If not, I'm sure they'll have something on the helicopter Jackson called for."

I gave him a smile and started to unzip one of the bags. "Thank you, Lee. This is really sweet—"

Spiderzilla unfolded itself and swaggered out of the large pocket on the backpack. It was the spider from the plane, and it was back for revenge. I froze, my muscles seized in terror.

Until it ran at me.

I scrambled to my feet, only to trip over my water bottle. My foot rolled out from under me, and I tumbled onto the coffee table. But the table wasn't prepared for me to throw myself on it, and one of the legs gave way, sending me rolling onto the tile floor.

Out of the corner of my eye, I saw the spider scurry across the floor. To be perfectly honest, I didn't stop to check which way he was scurrying, because just the sight of the scurry was enough to send fear through me.

Leaping to my feet, I sprinted into the tiny kitchen like an Olympic runner. My record-setting run came to a halt when the large gaping pocket on the lab coat caught on a drawer handle. I was yanked backward so abruptly I'm pretty sure my body split, and my soul kept on running.

My forward momentum had been enough to yank open the drawer, and when I was yanked backward, my back collided with the drawer, sending me crashing to the floor. All the strange kitchen utensils no one knows the purpose for had been crammed in the drawer, and I was stunned when none of the sharp, spiral, pokey things stabbed me.

Win!

With the wind knocked from my lungs, I lay gaping like a fish out of water on the cold tile floor. As I contemplated what I must have done for the universe to send the spider version of a terminator back in time to kill me, the hair-legged creature darted into the kitchen.

I staggered to my feet and called for my magic. My body burst into a human torch and flung fire wildly in the direction I'd last seen the spider. Lurching around the island, I tried to make a run for it, but my foot stepped on a piece of the ripped lab coat that now dragged along the floor.

Not eager to kiss the tile again, I threw an arm out and grabbed for anything to catch myself. What I grabbed was the handle on the refrigerator door. It flew open and smacked me directly in my stunned face, and again I found myself on the tile. This time, I saw the silhouette of the spider as he ran under the refrigerator.

I should have just waved the white flag of defeat, but I wasn't a quitter. I made it a point to die and get right back up again. With my fire already spreading up the sides of the cabinets and blackening the walls and my mates all scrambling after me, I decided the best course of action was for all of us to leave and just burn this lab to the ground. Isn't that what all mature, grown women do when a spider decides to move into their home and start leaving sticky butt-crochet creations all over the place?

The plan would have worked perfectly if not for the

automatic sprinkler system sensing the smoke and soaking the entire room. Blinking through the water pouring down my face, I pushed to my feet again and stumbled out of the kitchen as fast as possible.

In hindsight, I should have seen the next part coming a mile away. My feet slipped in the water pooling on the tiles, and gravity yanked me down. This time, Mace broke my fall, which was nice for me, but not so much for him. The sudden spray of water had snapped him awake, and he sat up, confused, just as I plowed into him. There was an audible crack as my knee connected with his cheek. The knock-out blow sent him back to the floor.

I scrambled off him and backed up to survey the utter chaos I was partially responsible for. Fine, I was completely to blame for what had gone down in the last sixty seconds.

Eight sets of wide eyes stared at me with mouths agape... I couldn't decide if it was from horror or awe. I didn't miss the way Trevor's hands were covering his crotch protectively, but I couldn't blame him for being cautious.

"You didn't die?" Knox gawked.

"What? Like it's hard to stay alive?" I tilted my nose in the air. "I will have you know that I am alive more often than I am dead."

The door to the room flung open, crashing against the wall hard enough that the handle left a dent in the wet drywall. Jackson burst into the room, his eyes searching the room for threats.

The water must have soaked the ceiling and weakened

it, because when the door hit the wall, the chains holding up one end of the eight-foot-long metal light fixture came free from the ceiling. With one side still hanging by the chains, and the other side now free, the light fixture came in like a wrecking ball and took me out.

I guess it was hard, after all.

I regenerated on the cold tile. Naked. I lay there for a minute catching my breath. The spider darted across the floor in front of my face, and I stopped breathing. Imp landed on the tiles and tilted her head at me curiously. Satisfied I was only pretending to be dead still, she hopped across the tile and ate the spider.

I gagged.

Dramatic. Idiot, Imp seemed to say inside my mind.

"Did you really just act like you were demon possessed because of that tiny spider?" Anzac asked in disbelief.

Willard snickered. "You should have seen her torch the plane when one chased her there. She blew through a steel wall like it was nothing."

Dagger whistled. "That's what happened to the plane?"

"It was the same spider! And it was massive." I tilted my body toward them and whispered, "It's stalking me!"

"Koala Bear, that thing was small enough to sit on a quarter." Anzac laughed in disbelief.

"Do you even hear yourself? A quarter-sized spider is huge!" I insisted, although he was wrong. That thing had been at least seven inches.

The men shook their heads, but their eyes twinkled. Deep down, they loved my nonsense.

"I was only a few doors down the hall during your bonding and didn't hear anything from this room." Jackson began to laugh, and tears ran down his cheeks. Finally, he gasped out, "It's sad that a spider made your mate scream louder than any of you managed."

*M*y stomach pitched as the helicopter navigated through a narrow mountain pass. Feeling chilled, I pulled a dark sweater over my head and tried to focus on Jackson. He was rushing to give us a rundown of the information he'd found out about the train. We thought we had two days before the train was supposed to take the speakers to the summit, but the plans had changed due to a snowstorm that had picked up speed and was blanketing the northern mountain range with several feet of snow.

With the attack timeline being bumped up, we had to move fast if we were going to stop it from happening. It was too late to call the delegates and scientists to let them know what was going on; they'd already boarded by the time Jackson hacked into the facility's computer to get the train's info.

Willard got in touch with the General, but the closest soldiers he trusted to send in were still hours away. They wouldn't get here until after everything was supposed to go down. We were on our own.

It had been a mad rush to grab our gear and board the helicopter, but we'd managed to get into the air less than an hour after Jackson had discovered the new timeline. I snuggled against Mace, trying to ease the anxiety making it hard to breathe.

"Ryls, you don't have to come. This is what we do." Mace squeezed my bouncing knee.

"I'm going. This is my fight." I wrapped my fingers around his hand.

Jackson handed me a phone. "This has all the proof I could find about the plan to cause an 'accident' for the train. It also includes documents and correspondence detailing the plans to create more of their Human 2.0 formula to bribe their way into leadership positions around the world. Hopefully this will be enough for the imbeciles to realize you aren't the threat."

I took the phone and tucked it inside one of the pockets of my pants. "Were you able to put together the documents I asked for?"

"Yes. I'm not sure you'll have the chance to use them, but they're stored on the phone as well." Jackson's brow wrinkled as he studied me.

I was saved any further questions by the pilot's voice in my earpiece.

"The train will be on a straight stretch of track in two minutes. Prepare to exit."

Even in the thick darkness, the pilot expertly maneuvered the helicopter until the landing rails nearly touched a train car roof.

"Move, move, move!" Anzac barked.

I prepared to jump, but Mace swept me up in his arms and dropped from the helicopter with me tucked against him. The helicopter lifted back into the air. The pilot and Jackson would follow the train the best they could, but the thick pine trees and curving train track would make it a challenge.

The men ran across the snow-dusted roof and dropped to the cramped landing between the train cars. Anzac opened the door, and we all moved from the biting cold into the cozy warmth.

We'd entered a dining car, and every table was full. Some with businessmen and businesswomen in perfectly tailored suits, while others held families with smiling parents and excited children. They were creating lasting memories of things they would talk about for years... but only if we stopped what was about to happen.

I searched the faces but didn't find the ones I was looking for. If I wanted to end this, I needed to go straight to the people at the top of the food chain.

We need to keep searching, and we need to get to the front of the train, I spoke through the bond.

The information Jackson had dug up alluded to the train's brakes being tampered with and a bomb being planted in the rail car where the politicians and scientists' cabins had been booked by the make-believe summit.

We needed to clear those areas of threats ASAP.

With no time to waste, we raced from car to car. I came to a stop when we stumbled into another dining car, and I recognized many of the faces from the files at the facility. They'd done extensive research on each of these people.

Mace and Willard, stay with Ryls. You two can provide backup if needed. They may feel more comfortable seeing a human with Ryls. Trevor and Knox, go check for explosives in the sleeping cabins, Anzac ordered through the bond.

The pure alpha vibes he was giving off had my heart thudding hard, but there was a part of me that missed the clingy version of him.

Let's finish the mission, and then I will show you just how clingy I can be, Anzac rumbled in my mind.

"Xerxes, Jett, and Dagger, you two come with me." Anzac didn't wait for their agreement. He began running toward the front of the train.

Mace, Willard, and I were left standing in the middle of the dining car, and every single person was staring at us. Well, there was no time like the present. I took a deep breath and stepped forward.

"I'm not sure how many of you will recognize me, so I will introduce myself. I'm Amaryllis, and I'm the phoenix everyone seems to be hunting."

Gasps echoed around the room, and fear settled onto many of the faces. Several of the speakers had brought their families on the trip, and I saw their arms tighten around their little ones.

"Please don't be afraid of me. The last thing I want is to hurt anyone. I've spent my whole life hurting and in pain, and it's not fun." I pulled an empty dining seat into the middle of the aisle and sat down. I hoped it would help them see I wasn't a threat.

"There isn't much time left, so I have to explain things fast. The summit was a hoax. It was set up by Ridgeforce to lure you all onto this train, making it easier to take out everyone who disagrees with them." Panicked murmurs rippled through the cabin.

"Listen to me. I'm here with my mates to try and stop this plan from happening." I pulled the phone out of my pocket and handed it to Willard, asking him to take it to the gentleman who'd been pushing the hardest for my permanent death.

"That phone contains proof of what I am telling you. I want you to see with your own eyes how deep the corruption goes. Read those emails where they plan your deaths, and don't care if they take out hundreds of innocent lives in the process. Then you can tell me who the real monsters are." I watched the man flip through image after image, his face growing paler with each swipe of his finger. He showed it to the person next to him and created a ripple effect of horrified faces.

"I've included my own document on the phone. It's a contract offering an agreement between the organizations that haven't proven to be corrupt, and me. I'm offering my help to take down these criminal operations. The contract also states I will work with your laboratories. I understand my blood may help with finding cures for diseases, and I want to help if I can. That's why I will allow blood samples and tests on myself, so long as I am treated with respect."

Glancing at the timer on my wrist, I knew I had to speed this up. "The agreement also states I will no longer have a price on my head, nor will I be hunted. That extends to my mates as well. My family will have the same rights and protections as any other citizen of the country."

A woman cleared her throat. "So, in order to have your help with the threat tonight, we need to sign that contract?"

I stood and pushed the chair back where it belonged. "No. I am here because it is the right thing to do. I've been through hell my entire life, but I refuse to let it make me bitter to the point I'd refuse to help someone in need. We are going to do everything in our power to save you tonight, whether or not you choose to sign my agreement."

The man looked up from the phone; his eyes were red from unshed tears. "Ms. Phoenix, you are a terrible negotiator. Right now, we would sign anything to save our lives and the lives of our children." He looked at his daughter, happily coloring on a napkin, oblivious to the danger we were in.

"I don't want you to sign because you were coerced into it. I only want you to sign if you believe we can work together to help each other." I didn't wait for him to respond and, turning on my heel, I headed toward the front of the train.

Trevor and Knox were in the next train car.

"Find anything?" I was almost too afraid to ask.

Trevor ran a hand through his hair. "No, we've checked

these cabins three times, and there are no signs of explosives."

Xerxes burst through the door at the far end of the car. "Ryls! Jackson reached out through the mental bond and spotted the explosives. They are on the bridge that spans the river. It's a nine-hundred-foot drop."

My stomach dropped to the floor. "They are going to blow up the bridge and let the train go off the tracks into the river?"

"Yes," Xerxes whispered.

Trevor and Knox cursed.

"There's more." Xerxes's dark eyes met mine. "The breaks are damaged beyond repair, and we are picking up speed. There's no way to stop the train."

The train was hurtling toward the river... toward the death of everyone on board. This felt like a cliché scene in a cartoon with a superhero who liked to wear underwear on the outside of his body. Only there was no superhero, only a girl who was an expert at accidentally unaliving herself and a train full of lives.

I looked out the window at the blur of dark trees blurring by, and I knew what I needed to do.

I raced outside and climbed to the train car's roof. Balancing carefully, I called for my magic.

"What are you doing?" Mace shouted over the whipping wind.

"I have to go see if I can stop the explosives from detonating. I want you to go find Anzac and try to find a way to slow the train. That might be the only hope these people have if I fail." I started running, pretending I was back on the white-sand beach instead of a snow-covered roof.

My magic crackled around me, and fire ripped from my back just as I reached the end of the car. Without hesitation, I leaped into the air and raced for the bridge.

I had just made out the silhouette of the bridge in the distance when a deafening explosion lit up the night sky and shook the ground. A blast of wind slammed into me seconds later, almost knocking me into a tree.

It was too late. I glanced over my shoulder to see the train in the distance. It hadn't slowed. I'd failed.

No! I refused to give up and just watch while a train fell into the river. With a surge of adrenaline, I shot through the sky, faster than I'd flown before.

Reaching the smoking bridge, I circled it while studying the damage. Two of the main rails had curled, bending at strange angles and creating a ten-foot gap in the tracks. If the train hit this part of the tracks, it would be thrown off the rails and career into the river.

But that wasn't the only damage. The explosive must have been strapped beneath the gaping and twisted part of the tracks, because the support beams crisscrossing beneath it had suffered extensive damage as well. Even if the main rails had been perfect, it seemed unlike this part of the bridge could support the train's weight.

Iron and steel. Both were things that became pliable with heat. Could I burn hot enough to heat the rails and support beams? I'd have to be fast, because they needed to cool and harden before the train tested their strength.

The magic slid beneath my skin, a reminder of the power I still hadn't called on. It was now or never. I called my magic and gave myself over to the power instead of fighting against it.

The change was swift. The air wavered, my power bending the world around me. My ears popped, and suddenly the world was in sharp focus. The scent of pine trees and ash assaulted my nose, and my ears throbbed with the shrill call of a startled eagle in the distance.

Glancing down at the sluggish river below, I nearly fell from the sky at the reflection. My reflection. I was a phoenix. I'd shifted into a full freaking phoenix, and I was huge.

Flapping my fiery wings, I made my way to the top of the bridge and landed on the rails just before they began to curve. Grasping one rail in each of my massive claws, I sent the power of my fire surging into the rails.

The metal under my claws began to heat and glow a faint red. I watched as the heat continued to rush along the rails. I walked down the rails and slowly pushed the bent part of the rail back into place inch by inch.

Hope flared in my chest. It was working! But I had to move faster. I sent another surge of liquid heat through the rails and molded the rail back into its original position. I melted the metal on the ends to fuse the rails together before turning my attention to the braces.

Dropping beneath the rails, I grabbed onto the cross-beams and sent out another burst of fire. A dark shadow passed overhead, and I looked up to see a black dragon circling overhead.

Xerxes? I asked through our mental bond.

The dragon screamed, sending out a stream of emerald green fire. Okay, I was taking that as a yes.

Was this supposed to happen? I didn't think dragons possessed a full beast anymore.

The dragon dropped down to land on the undamaged part of the tracks and shook his head with a huff.

I didn't know that Phoenix shifters could actually shift to a full phoenix, yet here we are.

Xerxes's dragon was of similar size to Trevor's gryphon,

and absolutely stunning. I couldn't wait to get home and admire him, but first, we had to finish this mission.

Xerxes, I need a little more time to fix the braces. If you hang onto the back of the train and slowly heat the wheels with your fire, do you think you could slow it enough to buy me a few more seconds?

The dragon screeched and lifted from the bridge with a hard flap of his wings. He moved toward the train at a speed I wouldn't have attempted my first time flying.

I called more and more magic. Heating and bending. Melting and fusing. When the train came around the bend, I had nearly finished and had moved to the top of the tracks to fix the last two supports. That's when I heard the steady thump thump of helicopter blades. I craned my neck, thinking it would be Jackson and his pilot, but the two heli-copters that came around the side of the mountain were unfamiliar.

These helicopters were equipped with heavy artillery, and they were aiming at me. I looked back at the train; it was slowing, but it wasn't going to stop before the bridge. I had to fix these last two pieces.

Imp flapped in my chest, battering my ribcage. *You die in bird body. Won't come back.*

Xerxes was heating the wheels with his fire and using his weight to gradually slow the train. When he saw the helicopters and guns, he roared in fury and prepared to launch himself at them.

Stop, Xerxes! Help me save them! Keep slowing it down. Please, I begged. My mind flashed to the little girl coloring on the napkin, and the children in the first dining car, their faces bright with excitement.

Willard, Jett, Anzac, Mace, Dagger, and Knox were still inside, trying their best to stop the train. Willard wouldn't survive the crash, and it was unlikely even the jaguars could heal from the type of injuries a wreck like this would cause. I would lose them. If I let go and saved myself, losing my mates would kill me.

Ryls! Get out of there! Mace bellowed into the bond.

A few more seconds... I finished the last of the repairs and threw myself into the air, just in time for the train to scream past me, ripping off a few of my tail feathers. I tried to throw up a shield, but I'd spent too much energy and power repairing the tracks.

Guns boomed, launching the missiles. It was too late. I'd known I didn't have time to save the train and get away from the guns locked on me. I'd made my choice. And I'd make the same one a thousand times over.

Xerxes, keep slowing them down. Don't let them die. Please save them. For me.

I heard the shrill scream of my gryphon and of the tearing of metal as he ripped into one of the helicopters. My protector to the end.

Bullets slammed into my body like a hailstorm. One after another, they ripped through my flesh and organs, causing irreparable damage. I didn't have time to shift to my human form, and I didn't even know how.

I was falling. My body grew numb, and the comforting heat of my fire turned cool.

Imp, go! I didn't want this to end for her, not if there was even a chance she could live. *Go to them!*

Imp refused, so I called my last strands of magic to force her to take shape. Imp's tiny claws clung to my feathers, and she pressed herself against my feathered cheek, refusing to leave me as I plummeted toward the ground.

Thank you for being my friend.Please, watch over them. She let go, her fiery body sparkling up into the air and sending a shower of golden glitter falling around me. It was beautiful.

I love you all with every fiber of my being. I sent the last thought to my mates through the weakening bond.

I'd fight with everything I had to come back to them, but I didn't tell them that in the bond. I didn't want to hurt them more if it turned out to be false hope.

My eyes closed, and my heart slowed. Peace settled over me.

Arms grabbed onto me, and Trevor growled. *If you are leaving, then I am going with you.*

It was the last thing I heard before death claimed me and turned my body to ash.

21

KNOX

It had been a setup. Ridgeforce must have suspected we would try to stop the mass murder, and they'd been prepared to use the opportunity to capture Ryls. Knock her out of the sky, and capture her when she regenerates.

They hadn't counted on her not coming back.

None of us had.

I hadn't even had the chance to tell her how beautiful her phoenix form was. None of us had known she possessed that ability, and I'd wanted to finish the mission so we could celebrate.

Just as the train had rounded the last curve and was about to cross the tracks, Jackson screamed through our earpieces. "Lee just called. His friend finished translating an ancient piece of a scroll Lee had collected. It talked of the phoenix's ability to rebirth, but then warned of the phoenix beast being vulnerable. He thinks she might be able to shift into a phoenix like you guys can shift into a jaguar. But if she does, she needs to be careful. If she dies in that form, it is permanent."

The information came three entire seconds too late.

Mace shouted through the bond, but it was done, and I'd watched her be shot out of the sky with a violent barrage of bullets.

I slammed my fists against the train car's glass window and screamed at her falling figure, while horror shredded my insides. Ryls's fiery feathers had turned gray as life faded from her body. Trevor dropped from the sky, diving toward her body. It was like someone snapped their fingers. One minute they were falling, and the next, they were gone.

The bond shook and quivered. I tried to reach her mind, but there was nothing but emptiness.

This wasn't happening. I cried out for her to come back until my throat was raw, and no sound came out. Xerxes had yanked the train to an abrupt halt, causing some of the cars to knock into each other and passengers to tumble to the ground. No one was hurt, but I didn't care if they had all died.

We ran from the back of the train car, shifting into our beasts and not caring who saw us. All that mattered was getting to the last place we'd seen Ryls as fast as possible. For hours, we scoured the river bank for any trace of her or Trevor, but there was nothing. They were gone.

My mate had died, and she wasn't coming back.

None of us ate or slept for the three days following that devastating night. Jackson brought in a search team to help.

Despite Lee's tearful insistence that she was gone forever, we couldn't stop searching. Every time I turned around a bend in the river bank, I expected to see her beautiful face and wild red hair, a quirky comment tumble from her beautiful plump lips, and her eyes sparkle with a hint of mischief.

'Sorry, I regenerated and ended up falling into a pit and dying again,' she would say. Or maybe she'd spin a story about how spiderzilla found her.

Then we'd all laugh this off as a close scare. Xerxes would fly us to another of his exotic homes. We'd finally get to spend time relaxing and worshipping our mate's body the way she deserved, and arguing about who got to shower with her.

That was the way it was supposed to be.

"She's not coming back, is she?" Willard choked out. I glanced over to find him leaning against a tree with tears streaming down his face. Dagger was to his right, his body shaking with sobs. As for the rest of my shadow, I didn't even know where they were. Last I'd heard, they spread out, checking caves, the bottom of rivers, anywhere and everywhere. Xerxes's dragon had taken to the sky, hoping to find her phoenix floating through the clouds.

We all knew, but we couldn't say it—couldn't bear the thought of this being real.

Eventually, we allowed Jackson to send a helicopter to pick us up from that riverbank and take us back to the facility where Lee had decided to set up his own lab. None of us wanted to leave each other, and no place felt like home without Ryls, so the facility was as good a place to sleep as any other. The facility had been quiet, each of us suffering in silence. We never had a conversation about it, but somehow, we'd all ended up sleeping in bunk beds in a single large room.

It was on the seventh morning after my world ended that I was awakened by an obnoxious bird trying to sing right outside the window. It wouldn't shut up, and I couldn't sleep with the noise—not that I was sleeping well, anyway. Anger bubbled up in my chest. Nothing deserved to be happy right now. Snarling, I stomped outside to scare it off and found Imp sitting on the windowsill of our room.

"Imp," I breathed, not quite believing what I was seeing.

With a happy trill, she flitted to my shoulder and snuggled against my neck. My eyes watered. Imp was a piece of Ryls, and seeing her again made it feel like Ryls still lived on.

Miss.

I froze. That wasn't my thought.

Sad.

Was Imp trying to communicate with me? "I'm sad too. It hurts so much I don't think I can survive," I whispered, voice hoarse and my body trembling with pain.

"That's impossible."

I jumped and spun around to see Lee's stunned face. My jaguar was barely responsive, and I'd not heard Lee come outside. Grief had dulled all my senses.

"What's impossible?" I snapped.

Lee ignored my tone, used to the mood swings we were suffering through. "The creature. Everything I found about them says they can't live without the host. They are tethered. If this creature—"

"Imp," I corrected him. "Her name is Imp."

"If Imp is still alive, then I don't think Ryls could truly be dead."

I knew for certain Ryls wasn't on Earth. The mental link was dark, and there was no mate pull in my chest, but maybe she was somewhere else and was fighting to get back to us.

One day, Imp pressed into my mind.

Hello dear reader!

I bet right now you're hoping that…

My eyeliner is never straight.

I can never find a matching pair of socks.

I have to get braces a second time.

My internet connection always fails when I'm trying to submit documents online.

All my white laundry turns pink.

I forget to cancel all my free trials.

I forget the punchlines to all my jokes (ha! I already do this!).

I always pick the bathroom stall with no TP.

Every sock I put on for the rest of my life is slightly damp.

Both sides of my pillow are always warm.

The chocolate chips in my cookies always turn out to be raisins.

All my FB notifications are @everyone tags.

My videos will fail to load but the ads will play.

Believe me, I don't blame you! I promise if you hang in there for the final book in the series, it will make sense.

Now, excuse me while I go find a good place to hide until the mob stops trying to beat down my front door.

You guys are the best!

Sedona

XOXO

ABOUT SEDONA ASHE

Sedona Ashe doesn't reserve her sarcasm for her books; her poor husband can tell you that her wit, humor, and snarky attitude are just part of her daily life. While she loves writing paranormal shifter reverse harem novels, she's a sucker for true love, twisted situations, and wacky humor.

Sedona lives in a small town at the base of the Great Smoky Mountains in Tennessee. She and her husband share their home with their three children, adorable pup, five cats, two pet foxes, chickens, three crazy turkeys, two cows, and over a hundred reptiles.

When she isn't working, she enjoys getting away from the computer to hike, free dive, travel, study languages, and capture the essence of places and people in her photography. She has a crazy goal of writing one million words in a year and spending six months exploring Indonesia.

Made in United States
Orlando, FL
22 May 2023

33325374R10129